S0-AKV-537

Pioneers

Judaic Traditions in Literature, Music, and Art
Harold Bloom and Ken Frieden, *Series Editors*

Select titles in Judaic Traditions in Literature, Music, and Art

Bridging the Divide: The Selected Poems of Hava Pinhas-Cohen
     Sharon Hart-Green, ed. and trans.

From Our Springtime: Literary Memoirs and Portraits
of Yiddish New York
     Reuben Iceland; Gerald Marcus, trans.

Letters to America: Selected Poems of Reuven Ben-Yosef
     Michael Weingrad, ed. and trans.

My Blue Piano
     Else Lasker-Schüler; Brooks Haxton, trans.

Past Imperfect: 318 Episodes from the Life of a Russian Artist
     Grisha Bruskin; Alice Nakhimovsky, trans.

The Travels of Benjamin Zuskin
     Ala Zuskin Perelman

Vilna My Vilna: Stories by Abraham Karpinowitz
     Helen Mintz, trans.

With Rake in Hand: Memoirs of a Yiddish Poet
     Joseph Rolnik; Gerald Marcus, trans.

Pioneers

The First Breach

S. An-sky

Translated from the Yiddish by Rose Waldman
With an Introduction by Nathaniel Deutsch

Syracuse University Press

A Yiddish Book Center Translation

Copyright © 2017 by Rose Waldman

Syracuse University Press
Syracuse, New York 13244-5290

All Rights Reserved

First Edition 2017

17   18   19   20   21   22   6   5   4   3   2

Originally published in Yiddish as *Pyonern Ershter tayl "Di Ershte Shvalb"*
(*A Khronik fun di Zibetziger Yahren*) (Warsaw, 1927).

∞ The paper used in this publication meets the minimum requirements of the
American National Standard for Information Sciences—Permanence of Paper
for Printed Library Materials, ANSI Z39.48-1992.

For a listing of books published and distributed by Syracuse University Press,
visit www.SyracuseUniversityPress.syr.edu.

ISBN: 978-0-8156-3504-8 (hardcover)
        978-0-8156-1084-7 (paperback)
        978-0-8156-5404-9 (e-book)

Library of Congress Cataloging-in-Publication Data

Names: An-Ski, S., 1863–1920, author. | Waldman, Rose, translator.
Title: Pioneers : the first breach / S. An-Sky ; translated from the Yiddish by
    Rose Waldman ; with an introduction by Nathaniel Deutsch.
Description: First edition. | Syracuse, New York : Syracuse University Press,
    [2017] | Series: Judaic traditions in literature, music, and art | Originally
    published as Pyonern Ershter tayl Di Ershte Shvalb (A Khronik fun di
    Zibetziger Yahren) Warsaw, 1927.
Identifiers: LCCN 2017005042 (print) | LCCN 2017006743 (ebook) |
    ISBN 9780815635048 (hardcover : alk. paper) | ISBN 9780815610847
    (pbk. : alk. paper) | ISBN 9780815654049 (e-book)
Classification: LCC PJ5129.R3 P5613 2017 (print) | LCC PJ5129.R3 (ebook)
    | DDC 839/.18309—dc23
LC record available at https://lccn.loc.gov/2017005042

Manufactured in the United States of America

Contents

Acknowledgments

I owe thanks to the many people who helped me as I worked on the translation of this book. For the support of this project, financially and otherwise, I am grateful to Aaron Lansky and the Yiddish Book Center, and their extraordinary staff who facilitated the publishing of this translation: Sebastian Schulman, Gretchen Fiordalice, and Eitan Kensky. My fellow 2014 translation fellows who read and critiqued portions of this book: Beata Kasiarz, Eitan Kensky, Helen Mintz, Harriet Murav, Sarah Ponichtera, Sasha Senderovich, Anna Elena Torres, and Ri Turner.

Ken Frieden, my mentor during my YBC fellowship year, went above and beyond his duty, reading, critiquing, and editing the entire text. I am also indebted to Katherine Silver for her meticulous editing. I feel lucky to know her.

Susan Bernofsky and my workshop-mates at Columbia University were the first readers and literary critics of this work. I warmly acknowledge this outstanding group of translators: Tenzin Dickyi, Alexandra Watson, Adam Winters, Laura Itzkowitz, and Meghan Flaherty Maguire.

Incalculable thanks, too, to Ruth Wisse for intro-
ducing me to this book and for her general wonder-
fulness. And to Deborah Manion and the wonderful
staff at Syracuse University Press for making this book
happen.

Finally, I want to thank my family, who constantly
inspire me to do my best work.

Translator's Note

I discovered S. An-sky in a footnote. This was a number of years ago, back when I was in college and reading a book by Nathaniel Deutsch called *The Maiden of Ludmir* as part of my research for a paper on gender. In one of the footnotes, I read something that intrigued me: a man named S. An-sky had conducted an ethnographic expedition in the early 1900s to study the folk traditions, stories, songs, etc., of shtetl Jews. He perceived (though he couldn't have predicted the reason) that soon these communities would be extinct and forgotten. In one of his efforts to preserve their culture, which he hoped to document for future generations, he created a book-length questionnaire in Yiddish for shtetl Jews to answer. "A remarkable and still untranslated work," read the footnote, "it consists of 2,087 questions addressing a wide range of life experiences and related Jewish traditions, ranging from pregnancy and birth to death and mourning."

More than two thousand questions on Jewish folk traditions?! How could I not be intrigued? I looked up the contact information for Nathaniel Deutsch and sent him an e-mail asking where and how I could access the questionnaire. I explained that since I am Chassidic and Yiddish is my first language, I would have no problem reading it. But as it turned out, it wasn't that simple. The questionnaire was on microfilm (at that time), and quite a bit of due diligence was required to access it. Inexperienced researcher that I was, it was easier to let the matter drop.

Years later, in my second year of graduate school, I was looking for a good project for my translation thesis. I e-mailed Ruth Wisse, asking for suggestions. Although she didn't know me at all at the time, her response was immediate and generous. She expressed happiness at the thought that more Yiddish literature would be translated and then offered several recommendations. Among them was the novel *Pyonern* (*Pioneers*) by S. An-sky.

An-sky! The man of the two thousand questions! I hadn't even known he'd written a novel.

Later, of course, the extent of An-sky's prolific oeuvre became clearer to me. The longer I worked on this translation, the more I learned; and the more I learned, the more I was amazed at all An-sky had accomplished in his relatively short life.

Like Zalmen Itzkowitz, the protagonist of *Pioneers: The First Breach*, An-sky underwent several transformations in his life, or rather, had several "changes of heart." From a young Talmud prodigy in the town of Vitebsk, he turned into a Russian populist so radical, he all but renounced his Jewishness, only to later energetically embrace his Jewish roots again. But unlike his wishy-washy protagonist, Itzkowitz, who tended to be dragged along with whichever social current was strongest, An-sky took up each new phase (and the activities associated with them), because he'd reflected on the matter and made an informed decision. When he was a radical populist *narod*, he immersed himself in that lifestyle, because he'd come to truly believe in its socialist politics. Though the lifestyle wasn't easy, he was willing to struggle for his ideals.

Later, when he returned to "Jewishness," he again threw himself into his new self with gusto, resourcefulness, and sincerity. Inspired by I. L. Peretz, he began to write in Yiddish again and translated some of his Russian works to Yiddish, including the two volumes of his novel, *Pioneers*. It was during this phase, too, that he conceived of the ethnographic expedition. His newfound passion for everything Jewish heightened his awareness of just how endangered its traditional, thousand-year-old culture and lifestyle were. Young people, influenced by the Haskalah movement, were abandoning religion. Many of them were moving from the shtetls to cities. Soon, An-sky believed, nothing would be left of the shtetl lifestyle. And so, with his usual drive and energy, he set about documenting it.

An-sky's ethnographic bent is evident in *Pioneers: The First Breach*, and it was this aspect of the novel that drew me in most. The novel's historical background, the birth of the Haskalah movement in Russia, is depicted through the lens of the ordinary Jew living in the shtetl. Just as An-sky would later study the customs of the "simple folk" during his expedition, not those of the rabbinic elite, he chooses these same simple people as the eyes, ears, and mouths of *Pioneers: The First Breach*. Without his realizing it, An-sky, the ever-observant ethnographer, was already creating a document of an archetypal community in a specific place at a specific time.

For me, living as I do in a community that has carried on the shtetl Jews' storytelling tradition, I received an additional jolt of pleasure each time I recognized some of the "stories within the story." Take, for example, an anecdote told in chapter 18. In this scene, some of the town's men, the rabbi's inner circle, are sitting around a table, drinking and schmoozing. The purpose of this klatch is to persuade Itzkowitz, who has been invited to join, to change his ways, to repent. But they can't come right out and tell him that, so they initiate a friendly conversation. At some point, they start discussing the new fashion of big city synagogues' hiring of cantors who lead the services using sheet music. "From sheet music!" one man mocks. "That's a whole other sort of cantor. That's the sort of cantor who sings in the synagogue today and goes where the devil leads him tomorrow . . . like, into theaters. Singing from notes!"

This comment prompts another man to tell a story. "Once, a cantor forgot the most important note in the middle of the prayers. He couldn't remember it, no matter how hard he tried. So he couldn't move ahead, and he couldn't go back. He was stuck—mute. His wife was sitting in the women's section on the balcony, and she remembered the note. But how could she jog her husband's memory? Anyway, she suddenly burst into song in that same tune he couldn't remember. She sang: 'If you do-on't know ho-ow to do it, if you ca-an't do it, do-on't undertake to do-oo it.' So, of course, the cantor heard the tune and was able to continue the prayers."

In the novel, the men around the table burst out laughing, and as I read it, so did I. I laughed because I'd heard this story as a child from my father, a lay cantor, except in his version, the wife's "song" is funnier. Perhaps—and this would make for a good anthropologic study—later storytellers "improved" the original version. The way my father told it, when the cantor couldn't remember the melody he'd prepared for this section of the prayers, his wife sang out from the women's section: "*Oy, du alte shtinker / Az du kenst nisht, farvus nemstu dikh unter?*" Which translates to: "Oy, you old stinker / If you're not capable, why do you undertake it?" In Chassidic Yiddish, *shtinker* and *unter* (pronounced *inter*) are a slant rhyme.

Another recognizable trope was the gender norms, and nowhere does An-sky zoom his writerly lens in closer than when describing the roles each gender, both as a group and specifically, plays. The first minor characters in the novel, the couple who own the inn, seem so real to the reader precisely because they feel so familiar. The husband is impatient, exhausted by money worries, and irritated by his wife, whom he considers silly and a nuisance. The wife, Chana Leah, though, is actually a shrewd woman. She is chatty, yet wary, "gently" interrogating her new guest, Itzkowitz, so that he would open up to her. In her own way, she is ambitious, but even as she decides to help Itzkowitz find customers for his work as a Russian tutor, she is also quietly plotting how to protect herself if the town turns against him.

Chapter 6 opens thus:

> For a long time, Chana Leah sat and pondered how
> to accomplish the task she'd taken upon herself.
> It was an extraordinary task, and not at all easy.
> Before anything else, word would have to spread
> that a writing tutor had arrived in town. Naturally,
> everyone would be taken aback and start gossiping
> about it. After that, she'd already know where to
> stick in a word here, make a suggestion there. Of
> course, she wouldn't set out to praise the tutor or
> persuade anyone to send him their children. Why
> should she take that upon herself? There was no
> telling what would come of this, and if things went
> wrong, she wouldn't be able to wash herself clean of
> the consequences, not even in ten bodies of water.
> Also, they'd immediately suspect she had a stake in
> it. Only subtly, between the lines, would she throw
> in a good word for the tutor.

An-sky's Chana Leah is the classic Jewish yenta:
prattles a lot, but is more conniving and cleverer than
she appears. She can't write or read (and isn't at all dis-
tressed by this fact), but she has street smarts. She is
the typical woman of the shtetl.

The gender stereotypes appear in even sharper
relief in the public sphere, especially in the scene in
the marketplace after Chana Leah has let drop the
news that a tutor has come to town. While the men
make no appearance—apparently, they have remained
in their shops—the girls and women all come running,
each outshouting the other in their curiosity to know
more about the tutor. One woman predicts impending

love affairs; another that the Messiah is coming. The young girls sneer at the old women's narrow minds, while their own minds become filled with romantic images of what this tutor represents. Only later, in the quiet of their homes, is the topic discussed with the menfolk. "There, along with the sighs and the groans, came comments [from the men] like these: 'This can't be allowed. . . . We must do something. . . . Why is the rabbi silent?' And so on."

The women and girls push for what they want, which is to study Russian with the tutor. And for a while, they attain their wish. But by the time the novel ends, it is the men who dictate the standards. It is they who decide that this tutor, and what they fear he symbolizes, is unacceptable, encroaching as it does on their traditional lifestyle. And it is they who take the necessary steps to remove this threat from their midst.

Translating this novel brought a world alive to me and gave me tremendous pleasure. But, as can be expected, I also encountered a variety of challenges. In addition to the usual challenges nearly every translator faces regardless of which language one is translating from, I had to find solutions to some difficulties that are specific to Yiddish and/or to this book. Here is a list of most of these challenges and how I dealt with them:

Spelling of Yiddish names: I transliterated Yiddish names as opposed to Anglicizing them. Generally, I used spelling that I thought would be most familiar to modern English-language readers.

Names/Relationships: The novel sometimes employs a hyphenated construction to indicate relationships (e.g., Gedalia's Mirel for "Gedalia's wife, Mirel").

The hyphen may mean child of, wife of, or husband of. To retain authenticity, I kept these constructions for the most part, except where I feared it would cause confusion for the reader.

Book titles: Most of the books mentioned in this novel are called by their Hebrew titles. As a rule, I added a footnote with some explanation and transliterated the Hebrew title, followed by its translation, the first time the book appears in the novel. In subsequent appearances, I used only the English translation. Unless it sounded too contrived, I also included authors' names, so that the reader can easily find information on the books, if interested.

Variations of synagogue: The novel uses various words for *synagogue* (e.g., *kloyz*, *beis medrash*, etc.). To avoid confusion—and because all these words were referring to the same synagogue—I used synagogue throughout.

Reb/Rav: The title *Reb* precedes many names in the novel, as it does in most Yiddish books. I could have translated it to Mr., but "Mr. Zalmen" would draw more attention to itself than "Reb Zalmen" does in the Yiddish. Consequently, I chose to retain Reb as an honorific in some of the dialogue only, but eliminated it everywhere else. The word *Rav* was sometimes use instead of *Rebbe*. To avoid confusion, I translated both as Rabbi.

Two Rebbetzins: The novel features two characters who are referred to as *rebbetzin*. One is an actual rebbetzin, the town rabbi's wife. The other is a teacher who teaches girls to read Yiddish. To avoid confusion,

I only refer to the former as rebbetzin. I call the other one a "girls' teacher."

Mother/Mommy/Mama: In direct address, I used the spelling *Mameh* instead of Mama or Mommy, as the former sounded too Southern to my ears and the latter, too American. My spelling sounds as the Yiddish would in the characters' pronunciation.

Dubrov: One of the characters comes from a place referred to by An-sky as *Dubrov* in some places and *Dubronov* in others. My guess is that the place is Dubrovnik. I've left it as Dubrov throughout for consistency.

Gedalye: Two characters in *Pioneers: The First Breach* are named Gedalye. Changing the name of one of the characters felt untrue to An-sky, but keeping identical names for both characters would, I feared, be confusing to readers. I chose to retain the name, but gave the characters different spellings: Gedalia and Gedalye.

Pioneers: The First Breach presents a portrait of the shtetl on the brink of transformation. It is an illuminating historical fictional account of a lifestyle that can now only be found within the pages of a book. Transporting a work like this—as well as those from other languages and cultures—into English is important both to the health of literature and to our collective humanity. I hope this novel will bring as much pleasure to its readers as it did to me as its translator.

Pioneers

Introduction

Nathaniel Deutsch

Every culture needs heroes. And the culture of Eastern European Jewry before the great disruptions and, ultimately, catastrophes, of the twentieth century was no exception. What was different, even radically so, however, was the typical profile of the heroes who populated the folklore, jokes, and, by the turn of the century, burgeoning modern Yiddish literature that comprised some of the most important elements of Eastern European Jewish culture. In her 1971 book, *The Schlemiel as Modern Hero*, the literary scholar Ruth Wisse argued that one of these classic Jewish heroes—or, perhaps, anti-heroes—was the figure of the schlemiel, whom she described as "harmless and disliked . . . vulnerable and inept. The schlemiel is neither saintly nor pure, but only weak."[1] Two decades later, in his essay "The Maskil as Folk Hero," Wisse's brother, David Roskies, identified another unlikely

---

1. Ruth Wisse, *The Schlemiel as Modern Hero* (Chicago: Univ. of Chicago Press, 1971), x.

hero in the Jewish literary canon, the Maskil or individual who had embraced what Roskies called "the glorious but failed revolution called Haskalah," as the distinctly Jewish version of the Enlightenment came to be known in Hebrew.[2]

Both the schlemiel and the Maskil make appearances in *Pioneers: The First Breach*, in the figure of Zalmen Itzkowitz, the book's hapless hero. That is, if we can call him that, for even by the generous standards of modern Yiddish literature, Itzkowitz strains the limits of this label, as the novel, itself, appears to admit, "The slight, skinny frame, the hesitant steps, and the timid appearance of the 'hero' who'd been anticipated with such impatience, surprised the shopkeepers [of Miloslavka]." Indeed, here is how *Pioneers*, in the evocative translation of Rose Waldman, first introduces Itzkowitz to its readers: "A young man of about twenty . . . skinny and slight, with a small black beard, a hunched back, and furtive eyes. He wore a short coat that was too tight, and his bare hands protruded from the sleeves, which were too short; his trousers were ragged and patched, and his shoes were badly worn."

Perhaps even more remarkable than this initial description is the fact that over the course of the novel, Itzkowitz will not be alchemically transformed from a proverbial ugly caterpillar into some version of a beautiful butterfly. Rather than going "from strength to strength," as Psalm 84 put it, or even from weakness

2. David Roskies, "The Maskil as Folk Hero," *Prooftexts* 10, no. 2 (1990): 225. Roskies's article focuses on An-sky and his work.

to strength, as a classic coming of age novel would have it, in the course of *Pioneers*, Itzkowitz goes from wretched to even more ignominious. And yet, in some profound sense, Itzkowitz—no thanks to him and even against his will—will play a heroic, if sacrificial, role in the greater historical drama that is the real subject of *Pioneers*: the creation of a viable modern Jewish culture for the Yiddish-speaking masses of the Russian Empire who, at the beginning of the twentieth century, still constituted more than 40 percent of the overall world Jewish population, despite two decades of large-scale immigration.

Among the key architects of this cultural project was the author of *Pioneers*, Shloyme-Zanvl Rapoport, or, as he became known to his contemporary readers and to posterity alike, An-sky. If Itzkowitz represents a case of the schlemiel as hero, An-sky's itinerant life recalls a different Eastern European Jewish type: the *luftmentsh*, or individual who appears to live from air alone. For years, An-sky lived out of suitcases, slept on friend's couches, and avoided the authorities because he never possessed official permission to reside in St. Petersburg (Jews from the Pale of Settlement needed a special permit to live in the city until the Russian Revolution). Yet, unlike the classic *luftmentsh* who fails to achieve anything because his head is always in the clouds, over the course of five eventful decades, until his premature death in 1920, An-sky accomplished enough to fill at least five lifetimes.

In addition to writing *Pioneers* and other novels, An-sky composed stories, articles, and plays, including *The Dybbuk*, which would become the most widely produced drama in the history of the Jewish theater and, in 1937, inspire a classic Yiddish film. An-sky also devoted himself to overthrowing the Tsarist regime in Russia, though when the long-hoped-for revolution finally came in 1917, An-sky, as a member of the Socialist Revolutionary Party, found himself on the wrong side of the Bolsheviks, and was forced to flee the country disguised as a Russian Orthodox priest. Finally, An-sky engaged in pioneering ethnographic work as the leader of the Jewish Ethnographic Expedition into the Russian Pale of Settlement where, for three seasons between 1912 and 1914, he and his fellow fieldworkers visited over sixty shtetls in three provinces, where they collected hundreds of Jewish folk traditions, took thousands of photographs, acquired hundreds of ritual and everyday objects, and recorded five hundred wax cylinder recordings.[3] Long before An-sky embarked on his groundbreaking expedition, however, he was already employing an ethnographic sensibility in his fiction, including *Pioneers*, which depicts many aspects of everyday Jewish life and culture in the Pale of Settlement, the western reaches of the Russian Empire to which a vast majority of its Jews were restricted until the Russian Revolution.

An-sky was born in 1863 in the town of Chashniki and raised in the provincial capital of Vitebsk, where

---

3. On the expedition, see Nathaniel Deutsch, *The Jewish Dark Continent: Life and Death in the Russian Pale of Settlement* (Cambridge, MA: Harvard Univ. Press, 2011), 11ff.

he spent much of his youth in his mother's tavern—a common occupation for Eastern European Jews—while his father was largely absent. As a child, An-sky received a traditional Jewish education in a *cheder*, though he was far from being a *talmid khokhem*, or accomplished scholar, and instead of devoting himself to studying the Talmud and other rabbinic texts as a teenager in a yeshiva, he threw himself into learning Russian and joined the local circle of Maskilim or enlighteners along with his friend Chaim Zhitlovsky. Unlike An-sky, Zhitlovsky was from a well-to-do family with roots in the Chabad-Lubavitch branch of the Hasidic movement. Like his lifelong friend, however, Zhitlovsky would later join the Socialist Revolutionary Party and become a key advocate for a Yiddish-based diasporist Jewish culture.

Anticipating the trajectory of his literary creation Zalmen Itzkowitz, An-sky left Vitebsk as a young man and travelled to a smaller town—in his case, Liozno—a traditional Chabad-Lubavitch stronghold, where he worked as a tutor while clandestinely attempting to spread the Haskalah among its youth. These parallels—and there are more—beg the question of the relationship between An-sky's own life and the narrative of *Pioneers*, a topic to which we will return. After being driven out of Liozno by incensed residents, An-sky increasingly came under the sway of the Russian Populist movement, and in 1885, having embraced the Populist ideology of "going to the people" (Russian, *khozhdenie v narod*) with the passion of a true convert, An-sky traveled to the Donbass-Dnepr Bend mining region, where he tutored workers, labored in a series of manual jobs, and launched his career as a Russian-language journalist.[4]

Like his Populist comrades, An-sky did not view Jews as a *narod*, or people in their own right, and he even appears to have accepted contemporary anti-Semitic stereotypes of them as a parasitic economic caste. In February 1892, for example, An-sky wrote to the Populist Russian writer Gleb Uspensky: "I see only one possible solution to the Jewish question: to remove from the Jews, in the most radical way, all possibility of exploiting the population, and especially to protect the defenseless peasant village from them."[5] It would

4. Decades later, An-sky would implicitly draw on the Russian Populist concept of "going to the people" when he decided to embark on the Jewish Ethnographic Expedition into the Pale of Settlement. Indeed, Simon Rabinovitch, "Positivism, Populism and Politics: The Intellectual Foundations of Jewish Ethnography in Late Imperial Russia," *Ab Imperio* 3 (2005): 238; 241, has argued that, "he [An-sky] remained a populist throughout his life."

5. As quoted in Gabriella Safran, "An-sky in 1892: The Jew and the Petersburg Myth," in *The Worlds of S. An-sky: A Russian Jewish Intellectual at the Turn of the Century*, ed. Gabriella Safran and Steven Zipperstein (Stanford: Stanford Univ. Press, 2006), 65. Vladimir Yochelson, another Jewish Populist who would later become a prominent ethnographer, shared this view, "We were incorrigible assimilationists . . . I must concede that Russian literature, while instilling in us a love for the Russian people and its culture, persuaded us also that the Jews were not a people at all, but a parasitic class. This appraisal of the Jews was widespread even among radical Russian writers and was one of the reasons, I submit, for our defection [from Jews and Judaism]." As quoted in Judd Teller, *Scapegoat of Revolution* (New York: Charles Scribner's Sons, 1954), 131.

take years of self-imposed political exile in the capitals of Western Europe, where An-sky lived from 1892 to 1905 and the emergence of two interrelated phenomena among the Jews of Eastern Europe whom he had left behind, to transform An-sky's outlook and convince him that not only were Jews a people in their own right, but that he should devote the reminder of his life to working on their behalf.[6]

The two developments that would most help to change An-sky's thinking on the so-called Jewish Question were: (1) the rise of Jewish nationalism, which found expression in a number of competing political movements in the Russian Empire, including the socialist Labor Bund, various forms of Zionism, territorialism, and the Folkspartey (which espoused a Jewish form of Autonomism), and (2) the simultaneous efflorescence of a new Yiddish literary culture rooted in Jewish folk traditions and championed by popular writers such as I. L. Peretz and Sholem Aleichem, among others. Looking back on his own life on January 9, 1910, An-sky acknowledged how different his outlook had become since he left Vitebsk: "When I first entered literature 25 years ago I wanted to labor on behalf of the oppressed, the working masses, and it appeared to me, mistakenly, that I would not find them among the Jews . . . Possessing an eternal longing for Jewishness, I [nevertheless] threw myself in

6. On this, see David Roskies, "S. Ansky and the Paradigm of Return," in *The Uses of Tradition: Jewish Continuity in the Modern Era*, ed. Jack Wertheimer (New York: Jewish Theological Seminary, 1999).

all directions and left to work for another people. My life was broken, split, torn. . . . I lived among the Russian folk for a long time, among their lowest classes. Things are different for us now than when I wrote my first story. We have cultural, political and literary movements. . . . I believe in a better future and in the survival of the Jews!"[7]

In the wake of his transformation, An-sky published a seminal Russian language essay entitled "Evreiskoe narodnoe tvorchestvo" (Jewish Folk Art), in the journal *Perezhitoe* (The Past), in which he argued for the distinctive, even unique character of Jewish cultural heroes, thereby laying the groundwork for the later work of scholars such as Wisse and Roskies on the subject. According to An-sky, "In Jewish creative expression, and not just in folk-poetics . . . the heroic epic is completely lacking, there is no parallel to the Iliad or the Odyssey, the Scandinavian Sagas or Russian Bylinas. . . . adoration of physical strength is completely alien to the Jewish creative tradition . . .

7. Moshe Shalit, "Sh. An-ski loyt zayn bukh fun di tsaytungs oysshnitn," *Fun noyentn ever*, 1937, 231. See also, Deutsch, *The Jewish Dark Continent*, 6–7. Gabriella Safran, *Wandering Soul: The Dybbuk's Creator, S. An-sky* (Cambridge, MA: Harvard Univ. Press, 2010), 142, has noted, "By 1909, An-sky had joined three Jewish cultural organizations . . . the Jewish Historical-Ethnographic Society, a Petersburg scholarly group [founded by the historian Simon Dubnow]; the Jewish Literary Society, a national coalition of literary and discussion societies that organized speeches in the provinces; and the Jewish Folk Music Society. He eventually also joined Dubnov's Folkspartey and traveled around giving speeches for it."

persecuted and deprived of rights and power, a fertile structure for heroic epic of their own was never created. Nor was there any reason to be impressed by the heroism and triumphs of other nations and their knights."[8] Lest his readers think that this sensibility had disappeared in recent decades under the influence of modernity, An-sky wrote: "If one turns to popular creativity [folk art] of the last period—the period of storm and rupture and the struggle between fathers and sons, a period in which the young turned their backs on Torah and religious tradition—we still find in the stories of the [Jewish] people the same tendency which characterizes the folk creations of earlier generations. The only difference is that the secular Torah, the Haskalah, has taken place of Torah . . . in the place of the rabbi or the zaddik—have arisen the student, the doctor, the professor, and the writer."[9] As a writer in this broader tradition, An-sky not only created characters who embodied these distinctly Jewish heroic qualities, he positioned himself—and, after he returned to Russia in 1905, was widely perceived by others—as a Jewish culture hero, in his own right.

An-sky composed *Pioneers: The First Breach* in 1903, while still living in exile in Bern, Switzerland. Surrounded by other Russian Jewish artists and political activists ranging from Bundists, on one end of the spectrum, to Zionists, on the other, An-sky

8. An-sky, "Evreiskoe narodnoe tvorchestvo," *Perezhitoe*, 1908, I, 278.
9. Ibid., 297.

participated in a hothouse environment that inspired and shaped his own literary creativity. Two years earlier, in 1901, An-sky had read the collected works of I. L. Peretz, which sparked his appreciation for the artistic potential of the Yiddish language, and, in the same year, at a gathering of Bundists, An-sky spontaneously composed a poem, "In the Salty Sea of Human Tears," which quickly became the party's anthem after it was published in 1902.[10] Reflecting his embeddedness in both Russian and Jewish cultures, An-sky initially wrote *Pioneers: The First Breach* (Pervaia bresh') and the novel's second part, known as *Pioneers* (Pionery), in Russian. Between 1904 and 1905, both parts were published in serial form in the Russian Jewish journal *Voskhod* (Dawn)—also called *Knizhki voskhoda* (Booklets of Dawn)—founded in 1881 by Adolph Landau in St. Petersburg.[11]

Later, An-sky published a Yiddish version of the two parts of the novel in the popular Yiddish daily *Der fraynd* (The Friend), which was founded in 1903 and, like *Voskhod*, was also headquartered in St. Petersburg until moving to Warsaw in 1909. While its five thousand subscribers made *Voskhod* the most popular Russian Jewish journal in the first years of the twentieth century, its appeal was limited to the relatively small

10. Safran, *Wandering Soul*, 100.

11. On the publication history of *Pioneers*, see S. A. An-sky, *Pioneers: A Tale of Russian-Jewish Life in the 1880s*, trans. Michael R. Katz (Bloomington: Indiana Univ. Press, 2014), viii; Safran, *Wandering Soul*, 104–5. On *Voskhod*, see http://www.yivoencyclo pedia.org/article.aspx/Voskhod.

Russian Jewish intelligentsia and their ethnic Russian sympathizers, including the writer Maxim Gorky, who praised *Pioneers* for "its astounding tension of the will to live."[12] By contrast, *Der Fraynd*, which was the first and, for a time, the only Yiddish daily newspaper published in the Russian Empire, was read by the Jewish masses. Indeed, Scott Ury has written, "Estimates—unreliable as they are in such circumstances—put the paper's daily circulation at more than 90,000 copies at its height. As a result, some researchers claim that nearly 500,000 Jews (roughly 10% of the Jewish population in the Russian Empire at that time) read the Yiddish daily or had the news read to them as copies were regularly passed from hand to hand or, alternatively, read out loud in informal, semipublic gatherings. The large number of its female readers helped support the paper financially and also marked the growing participation of Jewish women in the public realm."[13] It is the Yiddish version of *Pioneers: The First Breach* published in *Der fraynd* that Rose Waldman has translated into English for this volume.[14]

12. See Mikhael Krutikov, "The Russian Jew as a Modern Hero: Identity Construction in An-sky's Writings," in *The Worlds of S. An-sky*, ed. Safran and Zipperstein, 135; Katz, *Pioneers*, ix–x.

13. http://www.yivoencyclopedia.org/article.aspx/Fraynd_Der. For the place of *Der fraynd* within the broader history of the Yiddish press in the Russian Empire, see Sarah Abrevaya Stein, *Making Jews Modern: The Yiddish and Ladino Press in the Russian and Ottoman Empires* (Bloomington: Indiana Univ. Press, 2004).

14. In Yiddish the title is *Pionern: Di ershte shvalb*. For Michael Katz's translation of the second part of the novel from the Russian version, see *Pioneers: A Tale of Russian Jewish Life in the 1880s*.

Gabriella Safran has noted that the titles of the two-part novel "suggest the invasion of a country by a band of warriors, who first make a breach into enemy territory and then send a party of pioneers."[15] Yet, Zalmen Itzkowitz, the protagonist of *Pioneers*, is far from being a warrior—at least a traditional one. Instead, as we have already seen, he is both a classic schlemiel and one of a new generation of Maskilim, "fighting on two fronts," as Safran has put it, "to acquire knowledge of non-Jewish languages and secular sciences and to bring that knowledge to their fellow Jews and thus reform them."[16] Itzkowitz is also a tutor.

Like the schlemiel and the Maskil, the tutor—often suspect and rarely treated with respect by others—emerged as one of the stock figures and, in some works, unlikely heroes of modern Yiddish literature. Thus, for example, I. L. Peretz portrayed the hero of his 1895 short story "The Miracle of Chanukah," as a constantly put-upon tutor or, in Ruth Wisse's description, "an impoverished Jewish intellectual who supports his ailing mother by tutoring the children of the Warsaw Jewish bourgeoisie," only to have his employment terminated unceremoniously.[17] Similarly, in "What is the Soul? The Story of a Young Man," Peretz created a character who inspired suspicion among pious members of the Jewish community, yet also provided a service that was increasingly sought out by upwardly

15. *Wandering Soul*, 104–5.
16. Ibid., 105.
17. Ruth Wisse, *I. L. Peretz and the Making of Modern Jewish Culture*, (Seattle: Univ. of Washington Press, 1991), 42–43.

mobile Jews in cities and shtetls, alike. As Peretz put it, "The tutor was a great freethinker in the town, and the neighbors didn't trust him to keep the dietary laws . . . But . . . [the] mother wanted her only son to know how to write."[18] Indeed, in 1904, at the same time that An-sky was publishing *Pioneers*, Sholem Aleichem published his story "Hodel," part of the Tevye the Dairyman cycle, in which Feferel, a socialist revolutionary, tutors Tevye's daughters in return for eating with the family.[19] In all of these cases, as in *Pioneers*, the figure of the tutor appears as a humble harbinger of modernity in its various guises.

It is not surprising that An-sky, Peretz, and Sholem Aleichem, all shared a soft spot for the figure of the tutor, since all of them, along with the other giant of modern Yiddish literature, Sholem Yankev Abramovitsh (aka Mendele Moykher-Sforim), had served as tutors in private homes before they became famous authors (Sholem Aleichem even modeled Feferel's relationship with Hodel in part on his own successful courtship of his onetime student and future wife, Olga, or Hodel Loev).[20] As such, these authors joined a long line of modern Jewish culture heroes who had worked as tutors, beginning with the philosopher Moses Mendelssohn (1729–86), the father of

18. *The I. L. Peretz Reader*, ed. Ruth Wisse (New Haven, CT: Yale Univ. Press, 2002), 96.

19. For a discussion of Feferel's role in the story, see Ken Frieden, *Classic Yiddish Fiction: Abramovitsh, Sholem Aleichem, and Peretz* (Albany: State Univ. of New York Press, 1995), 170–71.

20. Ibid., 114–15.

the Haskalah; Salomon Maimon (1753–1800), who followed Mendelssohn to Berlin and penned an autobiography about his treacherous journey to enlightenment
whose literary descendants would include *Pioneers*; and
Moshe Leib Lilienblum, the Russian Maskil whose
influential autobiography *Ḥat'ot ne'urim* (The Sins of
Youth), Itzkowitz smuggles into Miloslavka and gives
to his erstwhile protégé, Elya, to read.[21] For all of these
men, finding work as a tutor was not only a way to eke
out a living and achieve personal independence, it also
served as a crucial step on the road from tradition to
modernity.

Contemporary readers of *Pioneers* may be surprised by the lowly status of Zalmen Itzkowitz and
his fellow fictional tutors. After all, based on common cultural stereotypes regarding the importance
of education in traditional Jewish society as well as
the numerous statements in classic rabbinic literature
stressing respect for teachers, one might be forgiven
for assuming that all Jewish educators, tutors included,
were held in high esteem. And yet, the irony is that in
traditional Eastern European Jewish society, teachers
of young children, in particular, including the melamdim (plural of melamed), who instructed them in the
basics of literacy and introduced them to the Torah

---

21. Eli Lederhendler, *The Road to Modern Jewish Politics: Political Tradition and Political Reconstruction in the Jewish Community of
Tsarist Russia*, (New York: Oxford Univ. Press, 1989), 87, has written, "In 1866, Moshe Leib Lilienblum, who made his living as a
private tutor in the Lithuanian town of Vilkomir, was left without
pupils when he was reported to be a heretic."

and other foundational Jewish texts, were not only frequently drawn from the lower classes themselves, but typically earned a meager income and were often treated with condescension.[22]

It is important to note that An-sky did not portray Zalman Itzkowitz as a tutor of traditional Jewish subjects but as a *shrayber*, or tutor, who instructed pupils and, especially, girls, in writing and reading in foreign (i.e., non-Jewish) languages. Thus, when Itzkowitz first meets Chana Leah, the proprietress of the inn where he will be staying in Miloslavka, he exclaims, "I'll tell you the truth about why I came. I came . . . I came to give lessons. I'm a private tutor [Yiddish, *lehrer*]." When his host questions him, "What do you mean, a private tutor?" Itzkowitz explains, "Exactly like it sounds. A tutor [Yiddish, *shrayber*]. I teach reading and writing . . . in Russian, I mean." A number of scholars, including Shaul Stampfer and Iris Parush, have examined the important role that *shraybers* played in the secular education of Jewish girls and, concomitantly, the spread of the Haskalah to Jewish communities in Eastern Europe. As Parush has written, "*shraybers* who taught the girls to read were among the vectors by which maskilic ideas were carried to the smaller towns,

22. That this reflected a deeply rooted historical phenomenon is suggested by Samuel Feiner's observation that, "Private tutors like [Moses] Mendelssohn were lumped together with servants in the least privileged order," of the six official categories of Jews in Friedrich II's Prussia. See Samuel Feiner, *Moses Mendelssohn: Philosopher of the Enlightenment* (New Haven, CT: Yale Univ. Press, 2010), 39.

and the girls who learned from them the craft of writing were exposed to such ideas, among others."[23]

Parush also quotes from several accounts written by Eastern European Jews who were born in the nineteenth century that provide important historical context for An-sky's fictional portrait of Itzkowitz. Thus, Ben-Zion Katz, born in 1876 in Lithuania (that is, roughly the same geographical region in which *Pioneers* is set), recalled, "One time an ex-yeshiva scholar who had decided to become a teacher came and instructed the girls . . . He brought with him maskilic books . . . and so, drop by drop, the Haskalah penetrated my town." Similarly, Alexander Ziskind Rabinowitz remembered, "These scribes [*shraybers*] were simple Jews, sometimes a trifle maskilic . . . They were not at all esteemed in the eyes of the people, who treated them almost with contempt, but they had nothing against them either, as they recognized the value of being able to write script, to sign some paper or to read some note. The scribe would collect a group of male and female pupils together and give them lessons for a fee. . . . These miserable paupers were the first to bring the Haskalah amongst the people."[24]

23. Iris Parush, *Reading Jewish Women: Marginality and Modernization in Nineteenth-Century Eastern European Jewish Society* (Waltham, MA: Brandeis Univ. Press, 2004), 69.

24. Ben-Zion Katz, *Al Itonim va-anashim* (Tel Aviv: Tcherikover, 1983), 11; Alexander Ziskind Rabinowitz, "The History of the Education and Enlightenment of Russian Jews," (in Hebrew), *Hahinuch* 3 (1913): 103–4, as cited in Parush, *Reading Jewish Women*, 69.

When it came to secular education, Jewish girls in Eastern Europe experienced what Parush has called the "benefit of marginality," insofar as they were frequently more likely than Jewish boys to receive at least basic foreign language instruction from a *shrayber* like Itzkowitz. This was because girls were not expected—or from a Halakhic (Jewish legal) perspective, commanded—to devote themselves to learning rabbinic texts in Hebrew and Aramaic and, therefore, they had more freedom to study material that was considered beneficial to them for other reasons (but which for men and boys was often derided as *bittul torah*, or a waste of time that could be spent learning holy texts). These beneficial reasons included added social prestige as well as the tangible economic benefits that came with being able to write letters, read documents, and keep accounts. The fact that many girls were encouraged to get at least a rudimentary secular education in order to perform these commercial tasks reflects an important dimension of gender roles in Eastern European Jewish society: the so-called cult of domesticity that largely relegated women to the home in Western Europe did not exist among traditional Eastern European Jews.[25] On the contrary, Jewish women were often expected to work outside of the home and, in those cases where their husbands were studying Torah full time, they were

25. On this issues, see Paula Hyman, *Gender and Assimilation in Modern Jewish History: The Roles and Representation of Women* (Seattle: Univ. of Washington Press, 1995).

frequently the only breadwinners and raised the children.

An-sky, whose own mother supported her family by running a tavern, was well aware of the crucial economic role that Jewish women played in their communities. It is no wonder then, that he populated Miroslavka with numerous working women, beginning with Chana Leah, the colorful innkeeper and classic *balebuste* (homemaker), who greets Itzkowitz when he arrives in town, provides him with room and board, and helps connect him to other local women who may want to employ a Russian-language tutor for their daughters. One such woman, Gnessa Yachnes, mentions to Itzkowitz that her daughter already has a female teacher or rebbetzin with whom she studies Yiddish, before adding, "To tell the truth, I'd really like my little girl to learn how to write Russian. It is necessary. In my shop." For their part, instead of viewing Itzkowitz with derision like the other townspeople, "most of the shopkeepers, young women and girls . . . embraced the news [of his arrival] happily. The word *writer* or *tutor* evoked in their imagination the image of a freethinker, a superior being—in other words, a hero."

Given the many parallels between An-sky's own experience as a Russian language *shrayber* and undercover Maskil in the town of Liozno and the plot of *Pioneers*, it may be tempting to identify An-sky with the character of Zalmen Itzkowitz. And yet there were also significant differences between An-sky and his literary creation. Whereas An-sky had mastered Russian as a teenager in Vitebsk and went on to be an accomplished author in the language, Itzkowitz "had only learned up to verb conjugations." An-sky had abandoned traditional Jewish education after cheder and, according to his diary from the period in Liozno, when his landlord commanded him to pray in the town synagogue, An-sky's obvious lack of comfort immediately drew the mocking attention of local children until they were shushed by the beadle.[26] By contrast, An-sky depicted Itzkowitz as a *yeshiva bokher* (student) before becoming a Maskil; impressing the residents of Miroslavka with "the thin, sad, mystical melody of the Gemara chant," and entering "the synagogue with the intimacy of one who enters his own home, where each and every corner is familiar. . . . Because of his ease and familiarity, none of the worshippers noticed his entrance. The only one who took note of the new, strange guest was the synagogue beadle." More differences, some of them major, between An-sky and Itzkowitz could be noted. But these would require revealing the ending of *Pioneers*. And that is something that you, the reader, will have to do on your own.

26. Safran, *Wandering Soul*, 23. For a more detailed analysis, see Gabriella Safran, "An-sky in Liozno: 'Sins of Youth' and the Archival Diary," in *Jews in the East European Borderlands: Essays in Honor of John D. Klier*, ed. Eugene Avrutin and Harriet Murav (Boston: Academic Studies Press, 2012).

Pioneers
The First Breach

1

A large, ungainly coach, a sort of Noah's ark stuffed with passengers, lumbered slowly and with difficulty down the wide, muddy roads of the town of Miloslavka. The pair of horses, so gaunt their ribs protruded, kept stumbling and swaying off course. The coach rocked and twisted like a ship in a storm, rose and dipped through inkwells of mud. Spattered from head to foot, the coachman—a small old Jew who looked fatigued to the bone—tried to spur on his horses, shouting and flailing his ragged whip with all his strength. At critical moments, he even cursed them, and his curses rang out like a howling prayer.

The coach stopped at one house, then at another. Moaning and sighing, disheveled passengers climbed out at each stop. Legs tingling, barely alive, they began pulling out bed linens, parcels, and cases of all kinds

Chapter 1 originally appeared in *Pakn Treger*, the magazine of the Yiddish Book Center (issue 72, Summer 2015), and was later reprinted in the *Anthology of Newly Translated Works* and in *Stories in Yiddish and English*, published by the Yiddish Book Center, Amherst, MA.

from inside the coach. Men, women, and children came running out of houses and shops to greet them, and the dead-silent street now rang with shouts of joy, kisses, and disputes with the coachman. Finally, the coach lumbered onward.

After dropping off the tenth, or perhaps the twelfth, passenger, the coachman peered into the coach, where a single person sat, huddled in a corner. He called out hoarsely, "Where are you going, sir?"

"Where am I going?" the man responded hastily, a touch of anxiety in his tone. "To an inn. Please be so kind as to take me to an inn."

"To Leivik?"

"Fine, let it be Leivik. I know no one. I'm not from around here."

The coachman groaned deeply and climbed back up on the coachbox. His plaintive sigh let the horses know they had to continue to plod. A quarter of an hour later, the coach arrived at a large, derelict one-story house with a door set in the middle of the front wall, beside which stood a tall post with a bundle of rotten hay tied to the top. As he drove into the stable, the coachman scrambled off the coachbox and shouted, "We're here. Please get out."

A young man of about twenty emerged from the coach. He was skinny and slight, with a small black beard, a hunched back, and furtive eyes. He wore a short coat that was too tight, and his bare hands protruded from the sleeves, which were too short; his trousers were ragged and patched, and his shoes were badly worn. On his head was a new silk hat, and on his breast, a grimy bib-front, sewn with black thread. The

young man looked around, bewildered: a long, deso-
late, empty street lined with haphazard houses steeped
in mud. On one side of the street, an old inn. The sky
thick with heavy, dark clouds.

The man grunted and stretched his bones. He
clearly felt uncomfortable and miserable in his tight
coat and trousers. He pulled a small linen pouch out
of his pocket, turned to one side, and began carefully
counting out some coins.

The coachman pulled the young man's parcel out
of the coach and waited for payment. Only now did he
have a chance to notice the man's unusual attire.

"What are you, young man? A singer?" he asked
casually. He couldn't imagine that anyone but a singer
would wear such clothes.

"No, not a singer," the man replied with a frown,
and turning back, he handed the coachman a handful
of copper coins. "Here's seventy-five kopecks, as we
agreed."

The coachman counted the money and said in a
woeful voice, "Sir, you really should give me a tip. You
saw the kind of trip this was! An ordeal! Have pity. At
least a gulden."

"No," the young man said, gesturing with his
hand. "I won't give you a single groschen more. Tips!
What a new-fangled invention! We agreed on the fare,
and I can't give you more, I'm not a rich man."

"Well, if you can't, you can't," the coachman said
bitterly. "I'm not going to take it from you by force.
May God be with you." Sighing, he climbed onto the
coachbox, and without wishing the man good health,
he drove off.

The young man opened the door to the inn: a large, gloomy, bare room with an earthen floor and a few dirty tables and chairs near the wall. The air was thick; the smells of liquor and raw fish filled the room. A middle-aged woman sat on a large settle, knitting a sock. When the young man entered, she lifted her head and her hands grew still, a questioning expression on her face.

"Good morning, ma'am," the man said, still standing at the door. "Is this an inn? Can a person get a bed here?"

The woman, not taking her astonished eyes off him, answered calmly, "Why not? Of course you can."

"For a few days?"

"Even for a month. That's what makes this an inn."

"How much for a night's lodging?"

"The owner will come soon and let you know. It won't be very much."

Satisfied with this answer, the guest sat on the edge of a bench and set down his parcel.

"What a terrible trip. Broke every bone in my body," he announced with a sigh.

"Where'd you come from? Far away?"

"Vitebsk. Been on the road for thirty-six hours."

"Did you come here on some sort of business?"

"Yes . . . uh, a rather particular matter," the guest answered.

The woman placed the sock down on the settle and stood up. "Would you like something to eat? There's cold fish."

The guest considered for a few moments, then nodded. "Might as well. Thank you."

Pointing toward a bucket of water in a corner, the woman said, "Go wash up. The washtub's in the hallway."

Once the guest had begun to eat, the woman sat down at the table and started to pepper him with questions: "Do you know anyone here? Have any relatives? Acquaintances?"

"No, no one."

The woman's drowsy thoughts quickened with curiosity. Who could he be, this young man wearing a short coat and an odd bib-like shirtfront who'd traveled so far and had neither relatives nor acquaintances hereabouts?

All at once she remembered that for days now Zelda-Glukl had been waiting for someone who was supposed to "have a look" at her daughter. Perhaps this was the bridegroom, and he'd deliberately dressed this way so as not to be recognized. Indeed, perhaps that's why he was so reserved and answered her questions so reluctantly. The woman was well aware that in such cases it was inappropriate and futile to interrogate the person; still, she couldn't control her curiosity and said, "Don't take offense at my question . . . but have you come here for a possible marriage match?"

The guest immediately understood what she meant and answered with a smile. "Ah, I see, you think I came to have a look at a girl? Well, you're wrong. I came here for a completely different reason." He quickly finished his fish and then became more lively. "I'll tell you the truth about why I came. I came . . . I came to give lessons. I'm a private tutor."

"What do you mean, a private tutor?"

"Exactly like it sounds. A tutor. I teach reading and writing." After a nervous pause, he added, "In Russian, I mean."

"In Russian?" The woman looked bewildered. "Who do you teach?"

"Anyone. Boys. Girls."

The woman, finding all of this quite confusing, thought for a while. Then she said, "So, you mean at a secular school?"

"God forbid. Who said anything about a school?" The teacher looked anxious. "I give lessons in private homes. Like they do in all the big cities."

"You mean like a girls' teacher? We already have a teacher for private lessons."

"This teacher," the tutor asked nervously, "does she teach only Yiddish?"

"Of course. She teaches the girls to read, even to write. But she herself isn't very good at it. Poor thing, she's an old woman."

"How much does she charge?" the tutor asked, still sounding anxious.

"How much? She charges whatever they give. Ten *komikes* a month, fifteen kopecks.[1] Sometimes, a warm supper. She's a poor old woman."

For a while it was quiet. Then the tutor asked in a hopeful voice, "What do you think, ma'am? Will I be able to earn a little something here?"

---

1. 100 kopecks equal 1 ruble. In 1914, a ruble was worth about 50 cents in US dollars.

The woman shrugged indifferently. "How should I know?"

"But still, what do you think? Look, you're a respectable woman in this town, may no evil eye hurt you. And you live here. You can probably venture a guess."

"Well, honestly, I don't really understand why anyone would want to learn all those things. Can't people get by without knowing?"

"What!? Think about it," the tutor said, trying to persuade her. "Think about the times we live in. You're forgetting, nowadays it's impossible to manage without an education. In times like ours, everyone must know how to read and write. In Russian, that is. At least a little."

"Everyone *must* know?" the woman repeated with a skeptical smile. She shrugged. "Thank God, none of us—not my husband, not me—knows the Christian Lord's Prayer. And still, may no evil eye harm us, we survive and make a living."

After a moment of silence, she added, "And, really, I don't understand. Who would take a boy out of cheder?"[2]

"The day is long. You can find an idle hour. And it doesn't have to be boys. I teach girls, too."

"Well, girls . . . I don't know. Maybe someone will send you a girl to tutor. Maybe you'll find a woman

2. A cheder is a traditional Jewish school for children, teaching Hebrew and Jewish religious studies.

who's—" She'd nearly blurted out, "who's *crazy* enough," but bit her tongue just in time.

The tutor felt discouraged by the woman's pessimistic tone and her lack of sympathy to his situation. He realized that any attempt to persuade her would be a waste of effort, so he chose a different tactic. Sidling up to her, he spoke in a calm, sincere voice. "Listen, the way I see it, you're a smart woman who understands how to do business. I'm sure you understand what I'm saying. I'm a stranger here, as you can see. I don't know anyone and no one knows me. Where should I go? Who should I talk to? How do I start? I don't know anything . . . Also, I want you to know that I'm not interested in all those modern things, those modern ideas. God forbid. I'm a Jew, and like all Jews, I'm trying to earn enough to make ends meet. We all have to live, and we all look for bread wherever we can get it, right?"

"Of course."

"So, I'm asking for your help. I don't want you to work hard, heaven forbid. Maybe a word here, a piece of advice there. Sometimes a word is more precious than gold. Needless to say, I wouldn't want you to go to all that trouble for free, heaven forbid. I'm not a rich man, but a few rubles, as they say . . . If things work out for me, I would, well, with the greatest pleasure. . . . I'd continue to stay here in your lodgings. God knows, it won't be a fortune, but still, something is more than nothing. And at the end of the day, we're all Jews. And we have to help each other."

The woman became more enthusiastic. The softness and warmth of the tutor's words made a deep impression on her. The offer of a few rubles brought the issue into new territory—a more businesslike, practical, and interesting territory—and she now answered with more spirit, "Well, well, why not? I'll try to help. Like you said, we're all Jews. But I don't really know how I can."

"What do you mean, how?" the teacher cried. "A few words from you will start me on my way. I don't have to teach you how. You'll just put in a good word for me to one or two townswomen . . . I don't need anything more than that."

And tilting his head to the side, he added passionately, "I'm not from here, and even *I* have heard about you. Your husband, Reb Leivik, is known far and wide. May all Jews be so lucky. A word or two from you will certainly accomplish a lot."

2

A middle-aged man with a disheveled blonde beard and thick eyebrows strode into the inn and bent forward as if he were about to punch a hole in a wall with his forehead. He stopped in the middle of the room, lifted his head, and looked around. Noticing the guest, he extended his hand and said mechanically, "Sholem Aleichem. And you, where are you from?"

Without waiting for an answer, he cried out to the woman, "Chana Leah, Vanka sold the flax to Baruch. May they both burn to ashes!"

"I told you—" his wife began.

But he angrily interrupted her. "*You* told me? A lot you understand! Stupid cow!" And he stomped off into the other room.

The woman stood up, put down her knitting, and calmly followed him. First, she asked him about the flax that Baruch had snatched out from under him. Then, nodding toward the room where the guest was waiting, she asked, "Did you see the young man sitting there?"

"Yes?"

"He's a tutor."

"What kind of tutor?" Leivik asked impatiently, preoccupied with his own thoughts.

"A writing tutor. He teaches goyish things. Russian reading and writing," said Chana Leah with an ironic smile.

"And?"

"He just now turned up."

"And?"

"He wants to stay here in town and get himself tutoring work."

"And? And? And?" Leivik yelled, infuriated.

"What are you *and-ing* about? I don't understand. And? And?" Chana Leah huffed. "No one can say a word to you anymore!"

"Why should I care about any of this? For what unearthly reason? Is it *my* problem? He came. Fine, he came. *Very* important for me to know. There you go again, mixing me up in the head!"

"Stop shouting and making such a racket. Do you think I don't have a good reason for telling you all this? Listen, he's promising me a few rubles to help him. Plus, he'll be staying at our inn. Now do you understand?"

Apparently, Leivik finally did. He thought for a while, creased his forehead, and tried to figure out how much the whole business was worth. "Pssh," he eventually burst out with disdain. "Not worth a hollow egg. How much can he earn here? Who will hire him? Who'll trust him with their children? Some kind of business that is! Teaching the Lord's Prayer! And anyway, the rabbi will chase him out of town. On the other hand, if he's promising you a few rubles, tell him

. . . whatever . . . And keep an eye on him. Does anybody know where he's from? Anyway, I have no time to bother with this nonsense. I'm going straight to Baruch to tear out his beard."

He passed the room where the tutor was sitting, threw him a contemptuous glance, and quickly went out the door.

Chana Leah returned to her spot, picked up her knitting, and, looking out the window at the branches, said slowly, "Have you maybe heard of Tzirel, Menachem Treines's wife, the Dubrovniker? Her husband deals in lumber."

"No, never heard of her."

"She has two daughters, and she's also raising an orphaned niece. Maybe she'll let you teach her girls."

"Is she a rich woman?"

"May both of us be so rich, even in ten years' time. She's the richest woman in town!"

After a moment of silence, she added, "You can also try Ephraimke's wife, Baila, another well-to-do woman. She has two boys and a girl. . . . Yes!" She suddenly thought of something, "I know who else you should go see. Chaim Isser's wife, Zelda. She'll be the first one to send you her girls. A little while ago, she told me herself that she wanted them to be able to write in goyish. She owns a big store, and many barons shop there."

The tutor listened attentively, devouring Chana Leah's words. As she listed about four or five other townswomen who'd be able to send their children to study, he began to feel more optimistic. "What do you think?" she said. "Maybe you *will* be able to make a good teaching job for yourself. It's possible they'll send you girls to teach, maybe even boys."

"Excuse me, ma'am, but do you have ink and a pen?" the tutor asked excitedly. "I want to write down the names of the women you mentioned. Tomorrow, God willing, I'll visit them."

When he finished writing them down, he handed the list to Chana Leah. "Please, take a look at my penmanship. I was in a rush now, but if I make an effort, I can write even nicer. I also write Russian very well."

Chana Leah couldn't write, but she peered attentively at the handwriting and lauded it properly. "A fine hand! Letters as neat as pearls. Pity I can't read," she added, without too much distress.

The teacher smiled at her praise and asked, "So, you promise . . . you'll discuss it with your acquaintances, you'll persuade them? You already know what to say."

"Of course, of course," Chana Leah assured him. "As soon as my husband gets home, I'll throw my shawl over my shoulders and go to the market at the town gate. Don't worry, I'll know what to say."

Wanting to win the woman over completely, the tutor glanced out the window and said, "It's time for afternoon prayers. Where's the town synagogue?"

"Oh, just a few steps away. When you leave the house, turn right, and you'll see it on the first little street."

The teacher quietly recited the end-of-meal benediction and left for the synagogue.

3

Zalmen Itzkowitz, the newly arrived tutor in Miloslavka, had become a tutor quite unexpectedly. He was
born in a small town. The son of a synagogue beadle,
he'd initially studied in a Talmud Torah, the community's Hebrew school. When he became an orphan at
the age of thirteen, he traveled by foot to the yeshiva
in Vitebsk with only a few kopecks and a letter from
the rabbi in his pocket. For six years, he puttered about
in the yeshiva, listened to lectures, and ate his meals at
the homes of different townspeople (a practice known
as "eating days"). He didn't always manage to get meals
every day of the week, so he often ended up fasting
unintentionally. His clothes were always ragged and his
feet were barely shod. The starving, unworldly, thor-
oughly boorish yeshiva life, the lack of a homey atmosphere or corner of one's own, the confinement within
the cold walls of the synagogue, marked Itzkowitz, as
well as most of his friends, with conspicuous neglect
and crudeness. Itzkowitz studied only out of necessity,
without any inner peace or enthusiasm, because he
knew that if not for his student status, he'd be forced to
go begging. His thoughts were always on the problem

of how to get more meals, and how to do so in wealthy homes where food would be more abundant. Cut off from real life by his daily pursuits, Itzkowitz, like his friends, lived in a world of fantasies and dreams—and not necessarily ideal or pure ones. Huddled around the smoldering synagogue oven, the yeshiva boys would spend long winter nights dreaming about lavish meals. And there would frequently be candid discussions about the joys of being intimate with women.

Itzkowitz didn't worry much about his future. He was sure the dean of the yeshiva would see to it that he wouldn't become an old bachelor. A bride, some poor orphan, would be found for him. And after the wedding, he'd obtain the only job available to him: as a melamed, a Hebrew school teacher. He never dreamed of being anything more than that.

And so it would probably have transpired, had he not become unexpectedly swept up in the winds of change blowing through at the time.

The winds of change: They came in the late 1870s, brought by the Haskalah movement, the Jewish Enlightenment, which was attracting large numbers of the Jewish mid-level intelligentsia. It was a remarkable period, and in many respects, a deeply tragic one. In the rock-solid wall of ancient religious-cultural foundations, a deep crack was forming. An entire generation of intellectuals were discarding the yoke of religion and flinging themselves toward the light: toward knowledge, toward a new life.

Zealous idealism (never commensurate with *actual* abilities and circumstances), the daring leap over a thousand years of culture, did not come cheap. The impulse on which the movement was founded was mainly to destroy the old, not to create a new national creed, and it put the entire existence of Judaism and the Jewish nation at risk. It left multitudes—nearly an entire generation—broken and crippled in its wake. They rowed away from one shore and never reached the other. But in and of itself, the movement's ardent idealism was beautiful; its breadth and daring were wonderful. A progressive movement originating from the people themselves, it initiated a new civic, nationalistic way of life.

Right from the start, the chief strongholds of the Haskalah movement became the yeshivas, those very institutions whose raison d'être was to protect and strengthen the ancient foundations of Judaism. Despite the yeshivas' strict regime and insulation from the world at large, they offered the ideal environment for the spread of heretical and enlightened aspirations. A number of thoughtful, intelligent boys—who, after all, lived in an atmosphere of spiritual nurturing—distinguished themselves by their inquisitive minds and perceptive characters. The yeshiva life freed them from family traditions and parental supervision, which helped them develop a sense of individualism and independence. Added to this, hunger, cold, and other physical privations awakened discontent in their hearts. For all these reasons, the yeshivas turned out to be the perfect breeding grounds for these winds of change. They produced the greatest number of pioneers, the first generation of freethinkers, and fanatical Enlightenment propagandists of any European educational system.

4

The first seeds of the Haskalah movement were brought to the Vitebsk yeshiva by a young man who wasn't a student but had merely visited and sat in on the Talmud lesson. This man, the son-in-law of the town's wealthiest resident, reckoned himself a genius in Talmudic learning, yet he was a secret Maskil, or follower of the Haskalah. He owned a considerable library of enlightened Hebrew and German books. Outwardly, he lived in the style expected of a son-in-law of the town's tycoon: he played the role of a diligent scholar who was financially provided for by his father-in-law. But he spent entire nights quietly reading books and preparing to escape this life, to go abroad and study in a university. As he got to know the yeshiva boys and discovered a few serious, capable ones among them, he carefully yet firmly began to lead them "astray."

He started with subtle disputations of the fine points of Jewish law, then engaged them in debate over subjects in the Talmud. Gradually, he sowed doubt in their minds about the holiness of the Torah. He lent them enlightened books, which exposed them, bit by bit, to new perspectives. Within a short while, the secret Maskil had acquired several dedicated students, who enthusiastically began to spread enlightenment ideas among their other friends. Before six months had passed, nearly half of the eighty students in the yeshiva had gone astray. As usually happens in such cases, the more reflective and knowledgeable boys pulled the lesser thinkers along with them, and they, too, became caught up in the general enthusiasm; they, too, were dragged along by the current. Among the latter was Itzkowitz. Having had no lucid, definitive religious conviction from before, he abruptly—without inner angst, without a spiritual breakthrough of any sort— sailed over to the other side. He became stunned and dazzled by the possibilities opened in front of him: *gymnasium . . . university . . . doctor.*[1] Everything he'd always imagined to be beyond the reach of an average person, everything that had until then seemed merely a beautiful dream, suddenly appeared attainable to him—he, the poor, hungry, contemptible yeshiva boy. Joyfully, he discarded everything he'd held sacred since childhood. He stopped praying and studying Torah and began instead to diligently study the Russian language.

The "Chabad center,"[2] which was actually a room off the side of the house of study where Itzkowitz

---

1. A gymnasium was a high school or preparatory school for university. For many Maskilim, leaving the fold meant abandoning yeshiva studies to attend a gymnasium (and later, university) instead.

2. The Chabad movement was founded in 1775 by Rabbi Shneur Zalman of Liadi, a rabbi of the Lubavitch sect of Hasidism. Chabad is the Hebrew acronym for *Chochmah, Binah, Da'at,*

and many other yeshiva boys lodged, was converted into a clandestine club for the enlightened ones, the Maskilim. Outwardly, everything remained as it had been. The yeshiva boys arrived promptly for their Talmud lessons. In front of strangers, they swayed earnestly back and forth over their Gemaras and studied loudly, lustily. But after evening prayers, once the beadle had left, the house of study became transformed. The Gemaras were hastily slammed shut and shoved aside. From hidden, locked boxes the boys pulled out prohibited books by Abraham Mapu, Isaac Ber Levinsohn, Mikhl Gordon, Moshe Leib Lilienblum, and Peretz Smolenskin, and equally taboo Russian textbooks.[3] The boys would pore over these till late into

---

"Wisdom, Understanding, and Knowledge." Although Chabad is currently known mainly for its outreach to secular, unaffiliated Jews, the original movement began as a novel approach within Hasidism, namely to counter the prevailing Hasidic ideology that God wants one's "heart" only. The Chabad philosophy argues that God wants the mind, the intellect—the interconnected wisdom, understanding, and knowledge—and through the mind, one gets to the heart. Shneur Zalman's seminal work, the *Tanya*, elucidates these ideas, insisting that "understanding is the mother of fear of love for God" (See *Tanya*, chapter 13). Translator's note: the "Chabad center" mentioned in the novel is actually called a "Chabad house" in the original Yiddish, but to avoid confusion with the ubiquitous modern-day Chabad house, which is used mainly for outreach purposes or to guide and help travelers all over the world find places of prayer and kosher food, I used the term *Chabad center*.

3. Abraham Mapu (1808–67) was the first Hebrew novelist and a significant figure in the Russian Haskalah movement. His most famous works were *Ahavat Tsiyon* (The Love of Zion) and *Ayit*

the night, sometimes even till daybreak. In one corner, a boy might be deeply engrossed in the examination of Levinsohn's *Zerubavel*; another might be swaying over a Russian grammar book. He'd recite ardently, in the same chanting intonations used for reciting Gemara: "*stol—stola—stolo—stol—stolam—a stolye!*" And again, "*stol—stola—stolo . . .*" A third would be studying Krylov's fables with the same fervor.[4] Others were writing their own articles or lessons. Every so often, these

---

Tsavu'a (The Hypocrite). These books are mentioned with much reverence by Elya in chapter 12.

Isaac Ber Levinsohn (1788–1860) was a key figure in early Eastern Europe Haskalah. His first and most important work was *Te'udah Be'Yisrael* (Testimony in Israel), which aimed to disseminate Enlightenment ideas within Jewish society.

Mikhl Gordon (1823–90) was a popular author and songwriter, active in the Haskalah movement, though he became disillusioned with its promises later in his life. Some of his songs, including "Di Mashke" (The Booze) are still sung in klezmer bands today.

Moshe Leib Lilienblum (1843–1910) was one of the most important Jewish writers of his time. His works and Maskilic positions evoked great controversy and helped form some key ideas about a modern Jewish national culture. His autobiography, *Hat'ot Ne'urim* (Sins of Youth) is mentioned in chapters 7 and 19.

Peretz Smolenskin (1842–85) was a prolific Maskilic writer and founder and editor of the Hebrew journal *Ha'Shahar* (The Dawn). His widely read writings helped consolidate a nationalistic Haskalah movement and Zionist ideology. His book, *Ha-to'eh be-darkhe Ha-hayim* (The Wanderer in the Paths of Life) is mentioned in chapter 12 with much reverence by Elya.

4. Kriyov's fables were the work of Ivan Andreyevich Krylov (1769–1844), a Russian fabulist writer whose works, mostly satirical, remain popular to this day.

activities would be interrupted by passionate debates on religious and philosophical themes, punctuated by legends and tales about the great Maskilim. At times there'd be a collective scoffing at the Gemara and the old pious generation, and often, there'd be outright blasphemy.

Despite the yeshiva boys' caution, vague rumors that heretics had infiltrated the yeshiva reached the ears of the dean. The rumors seemed to him so implausible and farfetched that he couldn't give them any credence. But when the rumors began to circulate more frequently, he started scrutinizing the students. He carried out an investigation, but when he discovered nothing, he relented. There was, however, a traitor: a yeshiva boy who had become a Maskil but then regretted his transgressions. He informed the dean of everything that was transpiring among the boys, especially in the Chabad center. The dean was appalled. He felt lightheaded, faint. For a long time he cried like a child. When he had recovered somewhat, he called a meeting of the town notables and pious members of the community, and they decided they would invade the Chabad center at midnight and carry out an inspection.

And so they did. Sometime around midnight, when the secret Maskilim were at an impassioned point in their clandestine activities, they heard clamorous banging on the locked door. Turmoil ensued. The boys hurriedly hid the prohibited books. But before they were able to purge the room of everything, the door swung open and a host of elderly Jews along with the dean stormed in. They searched and eventually uncovered everything: the heretical books, the handwritten notebooks, the Russian textbooks. In the boxes belonging to several boys, they discovered sausages and other non-kosher foods.

Not only were the yeshiva boys aghast, but so, too, were the inspectors and, particularly, the dean. His legs wobbled and he nearly fell onto the bench. He sobbed and whimpered like a child. The other men—as soon as they'd caught their breath—threw themselves upon the yeshiva boys with shouts and curses, and began beating them mercilessly. The wild scene ended with the boys beaten and bloodied, chased out of the house of study together with their boxes and torn books.

After this catastrophe, the yeshiva closed down. All the boys, even the devout ones, lost their meal allotments and they either scattered throughout the town or traveled back home.

The group of Maskilim who lived in town, both the open and secret ones, came to the rescue of the abandoned boys. They gave the boys some money and found them living quarters at the home of a Christian at the edge of town. Some were sent off to other towns with letters to the local Maskilim of those towns. A few of the younger ones found work with craftsmen. Others gave Hebrew lessons. But about five or six boys, Itzkowitz among them, remained without means, scraping by with the few rubles the town's wealthier Maskilim gave them each month.

Itzkowitz lived this way for one year. He studied because he had nothing else to do. He didn't travel at all the entire year. He studied reading and writing (he particularly worked on his penmanship) from a

Russian grammar text, in which he learned up to verb conjugations. In arithmetic, he studied up to fractions. In Vitebsk, where gymnasium graduates were offering lessons, it was difficult for Itzkowitz, whose knowledge was so limited, to find anyone to hire him as a tutor. So Itzkowitz decided to travel to another town. Someone pointed him toward Miloslavka, a large and rich town. There, one could not only earn one's daily bread but could practically rake in the gold.

At first he was scared to travel to a town and present himself as a private tutor. He imagined that wherever he'd land, they would stone him, drown him, eat him alive. But his hunger and need gave him courage. His friends acquired "respectable" clothing for him, collected a few rubles, and away he went. As they escorted him to the coach, they sent him off with good wishes: "May you turn all of Miloslavka into Maskilim."

"Wish me something better," Itzkowitz answered, only half joking, "that I don't return from there beaten to a pulp."

5

It didn't take Itzkowitz long to find the synagogue. As soon as he turned into a side road, he saw a large, old building with tall, grimy windows standing alone in a yard. Strewn about in front of the door were broken benches, scraggly branches, and clumps of sand, greasy with wax. Itzkowitz immediately identified the place as a house of prayer.

When he entered the synagogue, afternoon prayers were in full swing. They prayed rapidly, like people who'd torn themselves away from pressing work for a brief moment to repay a debt that must be hastily settled. From all sides came a stampede of words, like the brisk beating of a drum. The words' swift gallop was somewhat frightening. It seemed that if one of the worshippers were to stutter on a word or pause for just a moment, a catastrophe would occur, a collision, as when train wagons go off the rails. In their rush, the ensuing words would jump onto the preceding ones, then fly apart, and the entire prayer would turn into a pile of broken and mutilated words. Only the many years of habit had leveled out a smooth path for the words of prayer, and they flew with the swiftness of an express train without interruptions, straight to the heavenly throne.

Itzkowitz, who had spent his childhood and youth in synagogues and study houses, entered the synagogue with the intimacy of one who enters his own home, where each and every corner is familiar. He went in, rinsed his fingertips at the washstand, wiped them on the damp towel and, without looking around, went right to the stove and began to pray. Because of his ease and familiarity, none of the worshippers noticed his entrance. The only one who took note of the new, strange guest was the synagogue beadle.

Gershon the beadle, a short little man with a serene, naïve expression, always stood near the podium where synagogue services were conducted. From there he made eye contact with everyone who entered.

Gershon thought of himself as the synagogue's proprietor of sorts and so considered it his unequivocal duty not only to notice each new guest but also to question him in detail. He did not do this out of curiosity, but for several other reasons.

Most of all, if a stranger showed up at the synagogue, it was likely that some of the town's notables would later approach Gershon to ask him, "Who is that?" Such a question must, of course, be answered. And to ease the notable's curiosity, it wasn't enough to merely share with him the name of the guest. The notable would also want to know where the guest came from, what kind of business he was in, how long he was going to stay, and many other details.

Besides, there were other reasons why Gershon had to know precise details about the stranger: if a man came to Miloslavka, it undoubtedly wasn't just out of the blue. There was probably something here he needed. But it's not that easy for a stranger to find who he needs or make the arrangements he requires. Also, the stranger might be impoverished, without a place to sleep and stay. Who would concern himself about this person if not the beadle? And in order to tend to a person, you had to know who the person was and what he needed, didn't you?

The way Itzkowitz was dressed surprised Gershon, but he marveled even more at Itzkowitz's behavior. Usually, when a stranger came to the synagogue, he paused at the door and looked around, as if wanting to ask where to go next. Meeting Gershon's attentive-yet-tolerant glance, the guest would immediately understand that this was the beadle, would walk over to him, obtain his welcome greeting, and after a short discussion, both would know everything they needed to know. Itzkowitz, however, walked into the synagogue like a native and didn't even glance at Gershon.

Gershon looked at the guest and tried to recall whether the man had been here before. At the same time, he tried to determine who this young man could be.

He looks like a German! Like a wild beast! Where did he come from?

He was displeased with both the clothing and the behavior of the guest, and he summed up his outrage in one word: *Shegetz*! Insolent man!

He waited till Itzkowitz had finished praying, then went over to him, feeling like Mohammed when he went to the mountain that had refused to come to him.

"Sholem Aleichem." Looking offended, he held out his hand to Itzkowitz and faced him with an expectant expression.

"Aleichem Sholem. Hello to you, too."

"Are you a visitor?"

"Yes."

"Where've you come from?"

"Vitebsk."

"Are you planning to stay for long?"

"Hmm . . . I don't know yet."

"Do you have relatives here? Acquaintances?"

"No, no one."

"Did you come here for business?"

"If I came, I obviously need something here . . ."

"What kind of business?"

"Oh, too much to tell . . . something . . . some matter."

"Where're you staying?"

"At Leivik's inn."

For a while they were quiet. Gershon didn't take his questioning eyes off the guest, as if trying to hint that he should be more explicit. But Itzkowitz remained silent. Eventually, Gershon grew irritated. He gave a little shrug and asked dryly, "Will you come here often to pray?"

"Yes."

"Then you'll need a place to sit. Here, this is available." He indicated a vacant spot not far from the door. Then, as if he'd endured enough insult, he went back to his regular place at the podium.

Itzkowitz understood the beadle's mood well and smiled inwardly. *Sure, I'll tell him who I am and why*

I came, he thought. *And then before I have time to start doing anything, he'll ruin it for me. Nothing bad will happen to him if he waits a day to find out.*

Now a bit calmer, Gershon began to search for an explanation for the unusual guest's strange behavior. *Some people simply hate to talk about themselves*, he thought. *Go figure what kinds of people there are in this world! I mean, you can't hold a knife to someone's neck and say: "Tell!" And then there are some matters that are unbecoming to talk about. A marriage match . . . a permit . . . an exemption . . .* [1]

Gershon didn't understand the exact meaning of *exemption*. But he knew that when people spoke about it, they whispered the word furtively. And so he'd begun to use this word to explain away all the things that were unclear to him.

It was warm, light, and cozy in the synagogue, and Itzkowitz didn't want to leave. He stood at his table, opened a Gemara, and peered inside. After all, it was natural for him to mechanically open any sacred text in front of him. Also, this thought crossed his mind: *Let the synagogue beadle and the few men in the synagogue see me perusing a sacred text. It certainly won't hurt.*

The tractate was familiar to Itzkowitz. He had studied it just this past year. Turning its pages, he stopped at a difficult passage over which he'd once labored. He wanted to bring to mind the entire matter, all its questions and answers. But in the meantime,

---

1. *Permits* and *exemptions* refer to bureaucratic requests. An exemption likely implies a request to be exempt from military duties.

the worshippers had begun the evening prayer. Praying along with all of them, Itzkowitz still gripped the Gemara in his hand and became more engrossed in figuring out the enigmatic passage.

The ancient Gemara with its thick sheets and bent, greasy edges; the wooden, wax-spattered table whittled away in certain spots, attesting to broken fingernails; the quiet, fused hum of the prayers: the entire atmosphere of the synagogue evoked many memories in Itzkowitz. He hadn't been inside a synagogue for more than a year, hadn't seen a Gemara in all that time, and yet here he was again, sitting with one in front of a waxen candle. For a moment it occurred to him that nothing had transpired, that the entire year of his life in another environment with other interests had been merely a dream, and in truth he was still the same yeshiva boy as before. His heart filled with a warm sensation, a kind of nostalgia for something homey, tranquil, and lost.

Itzkowitz sighed deeply and bent over the Gemara. With intense thirst, he began studying the passage, exerting himself to remember the difficulties he'd had with the contradictions and the ingenious interpretations and justifications. Without realizing that he was doing so, he began to read out loud, intoning the traditional Gemara chant. Not once in the last few years had he studied with such enthusiasm, with such true fervor.

His heart suddenly opened to this familiar sacred text. Until this last year, his life had been bound up with this book, and all the melancholy, pain, and unshed tears that had gathered in his heart now spilled out in the thin, sad, mystical melody of the Gemara chant.

It was already long past evening prayers, everyone had scattered, and the only person remaining in the synagogue was Gershon. From afar he observed the remarkable visitor, and he felt more and more empathy toward him. How sweetly he was studying! The words of the Gemara filled his body, spread through all his limbs.

"Now *this* is studying . . . *this* I understand!" Gershon said to himself. "How is it that this man studies like an established householder, like a well-off member of the community who can reel off a page of Gemara after his prayers? This young man must be a great scholar, a genius . . ."

Gershon stood a short distance away and listened to the guest as he read out loud; he even forgot that he was supposed to go home and lock up the synagogue. He waited a moment. When Itzkowitz was deep in thought and grew quiet, the beadle tiptoed over to his table. After some hesitation, he blurted out with great deference, "I beg your pardon, mister . . . Is the lighting too dim? Should I light a new candle for you?"

"Huh? What?" Itzkowitz exclaimed, as if just awoken from sleep. "A light? No, thank you . . . I don't need . . ."

Gershon remained standing there. Since Itzkowitz didn't resume his studying, Gershon asked, "I beg your pardon. As I understand it, you're from a yeshiva. From a big yeshiva. Maybe from Volozhin or Mir?"

The question brought Itzkowitz abruptly back to reality. His idyllic mood vanished. He remembered that he was no yeshiva boy, that he was, in fact, a tutor, a Maskil, a heretic who had broken all religious boundaries. What had just happened to him here?

"What makes you think I'm from a yeshiva, from Volozhin or Mir?" he asked dryly. "I'm not a yeshiva boy. Just because someone studies some Gemara doesn't mean he's a yeshiva boy."

"Oh, I didn't mean to say, God forbid . . . didn't want to offend you . . . on the contrary . . . the opposite," Gershon stammered.

Itzkowitz closed his Gemara and looked around the empty synagogue. "It must be late."

"Nine o'clock."

"Late . . . peeked into a Gemara . . . found a familiar spot . . . haven't opened a Gemara in a long while," Itzkowitz said, as if excusing himself.

"But that's exactly how it is! That's the strength of the holy Torah! When you take it into your hand, it's impossible to tear yourself away," Gershon answered with a proud, happy smile. He paused for a moment, then added, "Earlier, I showed you a place where you can sit, here near the stove. But I just remembered. Along the south wall, a few seats away from the honorable east wall, there's an empty spot. The owner of the seat is traveling and will be away for several months. You can sit there."

"Thank you. But it's all the same to me," Itzkowitz answered. "Makes no difference where I sit. Good night." And he left for the inn.

6

For a long time, Chana Leah sat and pondered how to accomplish the task she'd taken upon herself. It was an extraordinary task, and not at all easy. Before anything else, word would have to spread that a writing tutor had arrived in town. Naturally, everyone would be taken aback and start gossiping about it. After that, she'd already know where to stick in a word here, make a suggestion there. Of course, she wouldn't set out to praise the tutor or persuade anyone to send him their children. Why should she take that upon herself? There was no telling what would come of this, and if things went wrong, she wouldn't be able to wash herself clean of the consequences, not even in ten bodies of water. Also, they'd immediately suspect she had a stake in it. Only subtly, between the lines, would she throw in a good word for the tutor. And she would do this not because of the few rubles he'd promised her, but because she really found him agreeable.

It seems to me, she thought, *that he's a quiet, refined young man. He went to the synagogue for afternoon prayers . . . He must come from a good family. You can see it in his face. A refined face.*

When Leivik came home, she flung a short jacket over her arm, and left for the market.

The market was located in a large open square, surrounded by taverns and the town's best homes. In the middle of the market were several rows of shops in wood huts, with short staircases up to the door. On that sea of mud, the huts looked like houses from a Paleolithic age.

Because this happened not to be a market day, there were no more than five or six carts in the market square, and the little shops were quiet. The shopkeepers sat at their doorways, knitting socks. From time to time, they flung comments at each other across the distance.

Chana Leah went into her cousin's clove shop. She asked her cousin how her children were doing, complained about her own health, and told her that for the price of six rubles, Leivik had purchased—pigs' hair! Suddenly, as if she'd just remembered something, she exclaimed cheerily, "By the way, there's news in town. A visitor. Do you know who?"

"Who?"

"Guess! I'd bet anything you can't guess. A tutor's come to town to teach girls goyish stuff. Oh, may I be so healthy!"

"What're you talking about?" the shopkeeper exclaimed, with some curiosity. "A tutor for girls, here? Oy, my dear, I can't believe it. I can't bear the excitement!"

She ran out of the shop and clamored to the other shopkeepers, "Girls! Come here quickly. Listen to this news."

From all the nearby shops, not only girls but also young and older women approached.

"Run, girls, buy paper and pens," the bearer of the news shouted again. "A writer's come to town, a tutor for girls, who's going to teach all sorts of goyish things."

This piece of news excited all of them. Questions abounded: "What kind of writer?" "Where did he come from?"

"Ay, she's teasing us," an older woman said. "What tutor? What kind of nonsense is this? She wants to make fools of us."

"I should be so healthy," Chana Leah interjected. "He showed up at our inn."

"Why would a writing tutor come here of all places? What are you talking about? Who is he? Whose tutor?"

A young woman, a daughter-in-law of the town's wealthiest businessman, approached the group. In a tone that seemed offended by all the excitement, she said, "Shh. Why are you all so shocked? Such unsophisticated people! Who doesn't know what a writer is? A writer is a tutor, a tutor who teaches reading and writing. Even grammar! In our town, Mogilev—"[1]

"In our town, Mogilev," a girl standing behind her whispered to another girl mockingly. She made a face and winked.

"Sickening to see how she turns up her nose at us," the other girl whispered back. "She thinks that just

1. Mogilev (or Mogilyov) is a city in Eastern Belarus. At the time this novel takes place, Mogilev was part of the Russian Empire and was a larger, more sophisticated metropolis than the primitive Miloslavka.

because she's from Mogilev, no one in the world is her equal."

"In our town, Mogilev," the young woman continued, "every child knows what a private tutor is. All the well-to-do families send their children to study."

"Even boys?"

"Of course! Boys and girls. A private tutor is no small thing! They're very well educated."

"Educated goyim! Apostates!" an older woman cried.

"Very well educated," the woman from Mogilev repeated. "Some of them are even graduates of the gymnasium, men studying to be doctors. In Mogilev, we—"

"Ah, enough with you and your Mogilev," another woman interrupted her. "Who doesn't know that in your Mogilev everyone is smarter than the next person? But Miloslavka isn't Mogilev, thank God. We can manage without this. A writer! For what earthly reason do we need one of those?"

But most of the shopkeepers, young women and girls—especially girls!—some of whom had already read "extremely interesting novels," embraced the news happily. The word *writer* or *tutor* evoked in their imagination the image of a freethinker, a superior being—in other words, a hero. Not brave enough, though, to openly admit their happiness, they tried to mask it with ironic comments.

"Here you have it. Miloslavka! A town like all others! With a tutor, even! What more do we need?"

"Now all the girls of Miloslavka will be educated!"

"Maybe educated, maybe not, but we'll certainly have some love affairs," an older woman predicted.

"Don't I always say it! No plague or misfortune ever passes Miloslavka by," a little old lady cried out. "No fire, no cholera, no conscriptions—where does it come first? Miloslavka! And now we got ourselves a writer."

"Ay, ay," sighed another. "The Messiah is coming. I tell you, it's time for the Messiah. A writer! Where did he come from?"

"Probably Vilna. Where else? He's a nonbeliever, clean-shaven!"

Here Chana Leah felt it was fitting for her to interject. "What are you talking about, my dear? Who's from Vilna? What nonbeliever? What clean-shaven? No, he's a young man like all young men. He's quiet, refined. May all Jews be like him! He arrived in the afternoon and went to the synagogue for prayers . . . and you call him a nonbeliever? Such frivolous chatter! Such nonsense!"

Chana Leah's words shocked the older women and they returned to their respective shops. The younger women then came alive. "Yentas!" the young woman from Mogilev scornfully exclaimed in the direction of the ones who'd left. "What do they know? They think everyone has to sit over a sock knitting all day or recite Psalms without seeing a living person in front of their eyes."

"According to them, it's all: 'just like a goy; an apostate!' That's all they know," another young woman said.

"Chana Leah, dear." A few sidled over to Chana Leah. "What does he look like? Is he young? Old?"

"Is it so important for you to know these things? Well, fine. Yes, he's a young man. Maybe nineteen, twenty, not any older than that. And dressed to the nines!"

Chana Leah genuinely thought the teacher was elegantly dressed.

Her comments aroused even more curiosity in the youngsters. "Oh, friends, I wish I could see him already," one of them exclaimed.

"I'm going to study with him," another one said, "as sure as I'm a Jewish girl. Chana Leah, do you happen to know if he charges a lot?"

"Very cheap," Chana Leah answered firmly.

"If it's cheap, I'll also study with him," a third said.

"Me, too!"

"Me, too!"

An hour later, the shopkeepers had already divided themselves into two teams, and the young were entirely on the teacher's side. The girls' hearts beat more intensely than usual. Warm, sweet dreams carried them far away from the muddy market with its weekly dreary routine. The older women, on the other hand, forecasted the saddest, darkest future, each one scaring the other with all kinds of frightening scenarios. They sighed, shook their heads, and repeated, "It's time for the Messiah."

At supper that night, the news was discussed among the menfolk. There, along with the sighs and the groans, came comments like these: "This can't be allowed . . . We must do something . . . Why is the rabbi silent?" And so on.

7

Itzkowitz left the synagogue in a strange mood. He couldn't understand what had happened to him. How could it be that he, the Maskil, the ardent free-thinker, would sit down in a synagogue and study the Gemara with such zeal?

He felt a bit ashamed of himself for his weakness. He forced a smile and tried to persuade himself that he'd deliberately done this to fool the men in town into thinking he was devout. After all, that was the only reason he'd gone to the synagogue in the first place.

This is good, very good, he argued with himself. *To be sure, let them think I'm devout; then they won't be scared to send me their children, even their boys . . . Oh, if they only knew who and what I am . . .*

He imagined how furious Gershon the beadle and the other Jews would be—Chana Leah, too—were they to find out how he'd been living this past year and what a dreadful heretic he was.

He smiled at how cleverly he was fooling everyone. But at the same time, he felt enshrouded in a soft, idyllic mood, his thoughts eagerly drawn to the topic he had just now studied. *So I've become a* baal tshuva?[1] *Returned to the righteous path?* he laughed. *Perhaps I should renounce my secular studies and again sit in the yeshiva with a Gemara. Ha!*

Back at the inn, Itzkowitz came upon a group of Jews who'd driven there from a wedding and had decided to remain overnight. They were drinking whiskey and tea and were happily frittering away their time. When Chana Leah spotted the tutor, she said, "You'll sleep in the garret; there's a separate room there."

"Sara'ke," she commanded her granddaughter, "take a candle and guide this young man to the attic."

Sara'ke, a ten-year-old girl, led Itzkowitz to the attic. Holding the candle as she walked up the stairs, she kept swiveling her head around to stare wide-eyed at him. In the room, she stood rooted to her spot as if enraptured, never taking her timid, inquisitive eyes off the tutor.

"Why are you staring at me, little girl?"

"Nothing." She blushed and looked embarrassed, as if she'd just been caught committing a crime. Placing the candle aside, she quickly ran downstairs and soon returned with a pillow and Itzkowitz's parcel.

Ill at ease, Itzkowitz untied it. Convinced that no one had touched or seen the terrible books that lay in there, he relaxed, and with a smile he asked the little girl, "Why are you staring at me?"

"Um . . ."

---

1. The term *baal tshuva* (literally, "master of repentance") generally refers to a Jew, formerly secular, who has embraced religious Judaism.

"Do you know who I am?"

"Yes!"

"Who?"

"I'm embarrassed to say," she replied, and covered her face with her hands.

"Don't be embarrassed. Tell me."

And he removed her little hand from her face.

"You're a writing tutor," she said bashfully.

"Do you want to study?"

"Yes," she exclaimed, and ran out of the room.

For a while, Itzkowitz sat there, a motionless smile on his lips. Then he stood up, locked the door, looked about him, and opened the parcel. Inside there was a white shirt, his tefillin, their case, and a small package of books tied with string: a grammar text; arithmetic, geography and history textbooks; and a book for pleasure reading. There was another package hidden within this one, separately wrapped in paper and tied with string. Itzkowitz carefully unwrapped this package, too. These were the hidden books: Lilienblum's *Ḥat'ot Ne'urim*, Sins of Youth; the first volume of Mapu's *Ayit Tzavua*, Hypocrite Eagle, and two periodicals of *Ha-Shahar*, The Dawn, in which was published the beginning of Peretz Smolenskin's novel *Kevurat Hamor*, Burial of the Ass. One of the freethinkers in Vitebsk had given all these heretical books to Itzkowitz as gifts.

He rewrapped and retied the heretical books and textbooks, put them under the headboard, lay down, and promptly fell asleep. He dreamed he was in the yeshiva and the dean was recommending as a marriage match for him the chunky, blonde girl he'd ridden with in the coach.

In the morning he awoke feeling refreshed and in good spirits. From this day onward, he knew, everything hung in the balance, and he was certain it would all work out for him. Taking his tefillin with him, he went downstairs and washed himself. Leivik, Chana Leah, and Sara'ke were sitting at the table drinking tea. Itzkowitz joined them as if he were one of the family, and asked Chana Leah cheerily, "Well, ma'am, do you have any news for me?"

"I went to the market yesterday. And to the shops. To tell you the truth, I myself hadn't expected your arrival to bring so much happiness. Looks like you were right, what you said about 'modern times.' All the girls were going on and on about how they want to learn to write."

"You don't say!" Itzkowitz exclaimed excitedly.

"Yes, indeed! Looks like you'll be quite successful here."

"Don't talk like a woman. Don't talk foolishness," Leivik interrupted her. "Girls babble. They're blabbermouths. And you repeat it. Think about it for a minute. Okay, so the girls want to study. But what will their fathers and mothers say? You think they'll give the children time off from the shops? What, are you crazy? And here you go blabbering and raising a person's hopes!"

"Maybe you're right," Chana Leah immediately agreed.

"Don't listen to her," Leivik said to the tutor. "All these things she's saying, promising piles of gold. Go to the wealthier householders yourself."

"Of course, of course. Yes, I see, I'll go myself."

"Now, if you were able to write petitions to the government, if you knew the law, that would be a whole other matter. Then you'd need all your writing like a hole in the head," Leivik said.

"Petitions? What do you mean? That can be taught. You can learn how to write like that," Itzkowitz began.

But Leivik cut him off with a mocking smile. "Really, you think so? Writing a petition isn't easy. It's not so easy to learn how. It's sometimes harder than learning a page of Gemara. Every word has to be in exactly the right place. If you put even one period in the wrong place, the whole petition is useless. It's no small deal, a petition!"

Without waiting for an answer, he stomped off into the other room.

After tea, Itzkowitz took his tefillin and, holding them in his hand, he said in a tone of uncertainty, "I should be going to the synagogue for prayers, but there's so much to do today."

"Well, what's the big deal if you pray at home," Chana Leah calmed him. "Leivik also prays at home during the week. A busy man . . ."

Itzkowitz allowed himself to be persuaded, went to a corner, and—earnestly, devoutly—he said his prayers. When he finished, he had a bite to eat. After that, he reviewed with Chana Leah the list of families he'd chosen to visit. She listened to him attentively, added a few other names, and accompanied him to the door, sending the greatest blessings his way.

In the market square, which Itzkowitz had to pass, they were waiting for him with much impatience. Among the women shopkeepers, the only talk was of the "writing tutor." Already, legends about him abounded. Several related that he was a great prodigy, the son of a rabbi, who had set out upon the world, insisting on learning all sorts of wisdom. Others declared him to be a dreadful heretic who'd fled from his wife, renouncing a large dowry. Still others quietly assured everyone that he was in hiding from military conscription. And so on. All of them kept lobbing curious glances in the direction where the mysterious man was expected to appear.

As he approached the market and saw the tens of eyes upon him, Itzkowitz panicked. Already he was feeling peculiar wearing the short, tight jacket he'd taken from a stranger, and now here were these countless curious stares. Added to this, he had to be extra careful as he walked over blocks of wood or jumped over bricks scattered throughout the sea of mud. He walked with bent head and hesitant steps, unsure where to place his hands.

The first shopkeeper to notice Itzkowitz called out excitedly, "Shh, quiet! Here he comes. He's on his way here."

The slight, skinny frame, the hesitant steps, and the timid appearance of the "hero" who'd been anticipated with such impatience, surprised the shopkeepers.

"Is *this* him?" one of them asked, astounded.

"So it seems."

"I'd thought he'd be a proper eyeful, something to look at . . . but he looks like some sort of a, well, a yeshiva boy."

"His looks are disgusting," a girl said passionately. "I wouldn't allow a writer like him to cross my threshold."

"Shh, what, do you want him to be made of gold?" another girl said. "He's a person, like all people."

"He's actually not even ugly. A refined face," a woman said, then added with a smile, "Upon my word, he's handsomer than Esther Nechama's groom."

"Writer!" a girl yelled out suddenly, and then hid behind her friends.

Itzkowitz looked about him anxiously. He was met with raucous laughter.

8

The first name on Itzkowitz's list was "Tzirel, wife of Menachem Treines of Dubrov," and in the margins he'd written the words, "a boy, two girls, and a niece." Actually, Chana Leah had said that Tzirel was the biggest miser in town—"a miserly sow"—but because she was also the richest woman in town, he had to start with her.

Tzirel lived in a big house with eight windows facing the street, and a porch. Itzkowitz passed through a dark foyer and entered a large room in a state of tremendous disarray with layers of filth on every surface. A dirty tablecloth hung over the table, touching the floor. It was strewn with the unwashed dishes of last night's supper and scraps of bread, bones, and other leftovers. A girl who appeared to have just woken up lay on a soft divan, wrapped in a blanket. When she saw the young man enter, she cried out in a frightened voice, "Mama." Cowering, she pulled the blanket up to her eyes.

"Who's there?" asked an irritated female voice from the other room, and soon a young woman with a flat, expressionless face and calf-like eyes entered the room. She was wearing a dirty dress, an even dirtier jacket with scuffed elbows, and galoshes on her feet. Even so, she wore three strands of large pearls around her neck. Seeing the unfamiliar man, she stopped in surprise.

"Who're you looking for?"

"I wanted to see . . . Does Tzirel, the wife of Menachem Treines of Dubrov live here?"

"Yes, that's me. What can I do for you?"

Itzkowitz tried to arrange his face into an obsequious expression. Taking a step forward, he spoke hesitantly but with a certain confidence. "I'm a tutor . . . you've probably already heard . . . your two daughters, may they be healthy . . . I heard you might want them to study."

"You heard that?" an astonished Tzirel said. "From who?"

"Chana Leah, Leivik's wife. At the inn," Itzkowitz answered a bit anxiously.

"Leivik's wife? That stinker, Chana Leah?" Tzirel repeated, even more astonished. "How do you like that! How does she know—the scoundrel!—what I want to do with my girls? When I see her, I'll spit in her face. What a lowlife! Where does she come off talking about me! Did she tell you about her cousin, the whore? She should talk about her, not me. You can go and tell her that."

Then, catching her breath, she added more calmly, "I don't need a tutor. My girls will manage. Go now, and be well."

The tutor rushed out of the house as if he'd been scorched, and stood rooted in one spot till he'd regained his composure. "A good start, no two ways about it," he said to himself with a deep sigh. "Ugh, to hell with her. Not for nothing did Chana Leah call her a miserly sow."

He glanced at his list. The second name was Gnessa Yachnes, three houses down the street. Upon reaching Gnessa's house, he met an elderly woman on her way out. She stopped and asked him, "Who are you looking for?"

"Gnessa Yachnes."

"That's me. You're the tutor, I imagine."

"Yes . . . you've heard?"

"Of course I've heard," she said with good-natured irony. "You're probably working up the nerve to ask me to send you my children? I understand. Poor thing, you've gone to all this trouble in vain. I have two boys, may they be healthy, and obviously, I won't take them out of cheder. And the girl is just a child, only ten years old, may she live to be 120. Anyway, the girls' teacher already has her."

"Well, the teacher! But she teaches only Yiddish, and I heard she knows nothing. I teach Yiddish and Russian, and if you want, even German. In our day and age, it's necessary."

Gnessa thought for a while, then asked hesitantly, "How much do you charge a month? Or maybe, for the entire term?"

"By the month. The price depends on what I teach, how much time I spend, and how many children are at the lesson. Usually, I charge . . . a ruble a month."

"A ruble a month!" Gnessa cried. "What're you talking about? I'd have to be out of my mind to spend a ruble a month on my little rascal. She isn't worth that much at all."

"If I get three or four children together, for only one hour, I'll charge less . . . much less," Itzkowitz answered, himself alarmed at the high fee he'd asked for. "I'll take seventy-five kopecks. For you, I'd lower that to fifty . . . I have to live off something, don't I?" he added pitifully.

Gnessa stood for a while, undecided.

"I'll think about it . . . To tell the truth, I'd really like my little girl to learn how to write Russian. It is necessary. In my shop . . . Do you already have a lot of students?"

"I've been almost nowhere yet."

"Well, go to a few other homes. If others send you theirs, I'll also send you my little girl."

Itzkowitz was satisfied with this reply.

Feeling that Gnessa was a good-hearted woman, he asked her, "Maybe you'd be so kind as to give me suggestions about where else to go?"

"Well, there's Menachem Treines's wife, Tzirel. She has two daughters and is raising a poor little niece. Between you and me, she's the biggest miser in town, but she's a rich woman. May I be so rich!"

"Anybody else?" Itzkowitz asked, not mentioning his visit to Tzirel.

"Go to Zalmen Isser, the flax dealer. He's not an exceptionally rich man, but he has a whole brood of children . . . who knows, maybe he'll send you a few."

Then she quickly walked away, wading through the mud with her big shoes.

Itzkowitz headed to Zalmen Isser, whose house Gnessa had pointed to from the distance. He walked in through the front door right into a large kitchen and found a girl who appeared to be about sixteen years old: a refined, well-proportioned girl with large, black, sincere eyes. At the sight of the tutor, she grew anxious and backed away, blushing, then quickly set down her glass of tea, and for no apparent reason, threw a rag over her shoulder.

"Does Reb Zalmen Isser live here?" Itzkowitz asked, a bit confused.

"He does . . . and you . . . you're the one who . . ."

"The tutor," Itzkowitz interjected.

"I know . . . Father's in the other room," the girl answered, staring intently at Itzkowitz. She held his gaze with her big eyes, as if to hold him there, keep him from leaving. And he stood stock still, as if he were waiting for something.

"So, you teach Russian?" she asked in a somewhat shaky voice.

"Only Russian. Obviously, I can teach Yiddish, too, but I don't bother with that."

"I would very much like to learn . . . but Father won't let me," she exclaimed bitterly.

"Why?"

"He figures that at my age it's already too late to learn and—that it's not proper. Also, he thinks I'm already educated and don't need to learn anything more. But all I actually know is how to read Russian. That's it."

"You know how to read?"

"Yes. A writer used to live in our courtyard, a clerk for the police station. His daughter showed me the alphabet and taught me how to read the letters. Afterwards, I taught myself on my own. We have Russian books that were left here by some sort of baron. I used to read them in our attic. I read through almost all of them, and now I can read well. But what's the use if I don't know grammar and can't spell? After all, grammar's the most important thing."

"Naturally."

"Is it hard to learn grammar? I think it must be very hard, that you can't learn all of it, not even in an entire lifetime," she said in despair.

"You mustn't think that," Itzkowitz reassured her. "Of course, studying grammar is difficult, but it's possible to learn. I could teach you all of Russian grammar in three months!" he added confidently, forgetting that he himself had only learned up to verb conjugations.

The girl glanced at him with reverence, and sighed. "If you only knew how much I want to study. I want to learn grammar and vocabulary. When I read, there are a lot of words I don't understand, and I have no one to ask . . . but I will study. Even if Father won't let you come to us, I'll go wherever it is, wherever you teach, and I'll pay you with my own money." Then she added, "Go inside to Father, discuss it with him. I have four brothers and three sisters. I'm the oldest . . ."

In the next room Itzkowitz found a middle-aged man with a full, straggly black beard and smart, cheerful black eyes. He was sitting at the table, adding on an abacus.

"Good morning. Are you Reb Zalmen Isser?" Itzkowitz asked.

"Yes, that's me," replied the man, peering attentively at the guest. "What do you want?"

"I'm a tutor. I wanted—" Itzkowitz began.

But Zalmen Isser interrupted his words, and in a good-natured voice, said, "Aha, so you're the tutor! Welcome. How are you? Take a seat."

Itzkowitz sat down.

"So, I take it you came to Miloslavka to teach children writing and grammar?"

"Yes, exactly."

"Well. And heresy, too? Come on, admit it! Don't they say all tutors are ardent heretics?" Zalmen Isser asked with an affable smile.

"God forbid!" Itzkowitz cried, frightened. "I swear to you, I'm no heretic. I'm a Jew like any other Jew. What, isn't a faithful Jew allowed to be knowledgeable in worldly studies?"

"Exactly! That's what I always say!" Zalmen Isser agreed. "For example, my oldest daughter, may she be healthy, also knows how to read the black marks on a page. She reads Russian—I tell you—fluently, like a stream. No worse than the best teacher. And, thank God, she doesn't know anything about heresy . . . So, where are you from?"

"Vitebsk."

"You don't say!" Zalmen Isser said, excited. "My city! I'm a Vitebsker, too. Do you know people there? Perhaps you know Reb Velvele Elkes?"

"Of course! Reb Velvele Elkes? Who doesn't know him? He's one of the most respected Jews in Vitebsk!"

"He's my uncle."

"Really? Well, then you must know he arranged a match for his youngest."

"Is that so!?" Zalmen Isser grew even more excited. "This is the first I've heard of it. He hasn't written me about any of this."

Walking over to the door of the inner room, he called loudly, "Faiga, did you hear the news? Uncle Velvele made a match for Nachman."

"Mazel tov!" a female voice was heard from inside. "Who with? Do you know?"

"Who did he make a match with? Do you know?" Zalmen Isser repeated to Itzkowitz.

"I don't know who she is, but the family is from Škłoŭ. A magnificent match, they say. With the most illustrious family. A dowry of eight hundred rubles and five years of financial support."

This, too, Zalmen Isser repeated to his wife. Then he asked, "And Reb Hershele the rabbinical judge? I'm guessing you know him, too? He's my wife's second cousin."

For a full half-hour Zalmen Isser asked about acquaintances and relatives, and Itzkowitz answered enthusiastically, regaling him with details. He waited for an opportune moment, then returned to the question that interested him: "So, Reb Zalmen Isser, what can you tell me about your children, may they be healthy?"

"Which children?" Zalmen Isser didn't understand.

"What I mean is, I wanted to ask you about tutoring them."

"Hmm," Zalmen Isser made a motion with his hand. "Tutoring! I have a herd of eight, thank God.

What, you think I should send them all to study?"
Then he added more seriously, "Obviously, in such
times as these, they should study. But where, oh where,
would the money come from, my friend? Oh, money,
money, money."

"God knows it doesn't cost that much."

"How much do you charge per month?"

"Eh . . . we'll come to an agreement . . . But first,
you have to be willing."

Zalmen Isser thought for a while.

"To tell you the truth, I'd thought my oldest
daughter would teach the others. She can read, I tell
you, how well she reads! It gives you a fright to hear.
Ettel, come here!"

Ettel came in.

"Get a book and show the teacher how you read."

Ettel left the room and returned immediately
with a crinkled issue of the *Sovremennik* monthly[1] and
began to read quickly and inaccurately, without into-
nation and with no concern for punctuation.

"You hear? You hear?" her father cried triumphantly. "She reads like a minister, doesn't she?"

"Yes, she reads very well," the teacher praised
her authoritatively, "but still, she would have to learn
grammar."

"Grammar?" wondered Zalmen Isser. "What do you
mean, she doesn't know grammar? You don't, Ettel?"

---

1. The *Sovremennik* was a Russian literary, political magazine,
originally published quarterly then later, monthly. It was published
from 1836 to 1866. It included works by Nikolai Gogol, among
others, and translations of Dickens's and George Sands's works.

"No, grammar is very difficult," Ettel replied quietly.

"Very difficult," Itzkowitz affirmed.

"Well, it's impossible to be educated in every subject," Zalmen Isser placated himself. "For her needs, what she already knows is sufficient . . . But how well she reads! Eh?"

"She reads excellently."

Ettel took the book and left the room silently.

"Sits and reads for days," Zalmen Isser said. "I have some books that I once bought for scrap paper from a peasant, and they ended up floating around in my attic. She found them and read through all of them."

He thought for a while, then added, "Listen. Go to the other houses, cobble together some children, and then we'll see . . . I'll probably send you the two younger girls. Maybe even one of the boys . . . I'll think about it . . ."

"But, the older one? It's very important for her to learn grammar."

"Grammar?" Zalmen Isser thought for a bit, then made a decisive gesture with his hand. "All right. I'll discuss it with my wife and decide. I'll probably send you the older one, too. May she also know grammar. If she's already so learned, let her be learned in everything! Come back in a few days."

♖

Itzkowitz left Zalmen Isser feeling uplifted. The friendly reception, the discussion about Vitebsk, the meeting with the charming girl who'd looked at him with so much admiration, and Zalmen Isser's promise to send him his children—all of this encouraged Itzkowitz and gave him hope.

In the next house, Itzkowitz met an old hunched woman wearing a scarf knotted over her forehead. In answer to his question whether Ephraim's wife, Baila, lived there, the old woman answered grumpily, "Why do you need Ephraim's Baila? She'll be here soon."

When Baila arrived, he informed her he was a tutor, but she cut him off right at the start. "Already heard. Great news. But if you hadn't come, nobody would have cried, either."

"Gets himself dressed up like a Purim actor and goes traipsing from house to house," the old woman added crossly.

"Go away, good-bye, go!" Baila said, and disappeared into the other room.

Itzkowitz rushed out of the house and went to the remaining houses on his list. In one of them, the mistress of the house wasn't home. In another, they wouldn't even let him in, explaining: "Isn't it enough that we tear off our skin to be able to pay the Hebrew teacher? Now, something new! Do you think all of us here in Miloslavka are Rothschilds!? Well, you're wrong there."

After lunch Itzkowitz went to Mendel Kazanov, whom Chana Leah had called "a man of the world." He found Kazanov with his wife in their shop, buying oats from a peasant. A young girl stood nearby. Seeing the teacher, she tugged at her mother's sleeve and said quietly, "Mameh, Mameh, the tutor's here. Listen. It's the writer!"

The mother threw a hasty glance at Itzkowitz and answered dryly, "Fine, fine, I hear. I'm not deaf. Let him wait for a bit."

The girl tugged at her father's sleeve and repeated the news item.

"Leave me alone," her father barked at her.

Once he completed the oats deal, Kazanov extended his hand to Itzkowitz. "How are you? So you're the tutor? What do you teach?"

"Everything," Itzkowitz replied. "Writing, reading, mathematics."

"Grammar, too?"

"Why not? With pleasure. But even before grammar, there's plenty to learn."

"I know that," Kazonov answered earnestly. After a brief pause, he asked, "How much time will it take to teach all this?"

"It depends mainly on the student . . . and also, you understand this yourself: the more you learn, the more you can—"

"So you're saying that secular wisdom is also limitless? Are you comparing it to the Torah?"

"Well, let's say it does have a limit."

"But it's important to reach the *right* limit, right?" Kazanov smiled. Then, turning to his wife, he asked seriously, "What do you say, Devorah?"

"What should I say?" Devorah answered, irritated. "I say it's a waste of money. But you don't listen to me anyway."

"Listen," Kazanov began to persuade her. "Nowadays, if you run a business . . . you sometimes have to write—"

"You can manage without it," Devorah cut in sharply.

"Mameh," the girl begged.

"Quiet! Shush," her mother yelled at her. "She also comes poking in with her opinion. Go! Into the house!"

"Do you maybe have something you wrote? I'd like to see your penmanship," Kazanov asked the tutor.

"Of course! Here."

Itzkowitz took out a small piece of paper. Earlier, he'd written several lines in Yiddish and in Russian. He handed it to Kazanov.

Kazanov took it and strained to read it. "Pa-pri-gunia strekoza . . . What does this mean, *paprigunia strekoza?*"[2]

"*Paprigunia* means, uh, something that jumps, and *strekoza* is . . . sort of, this type of little animal . . . you understand?"

"Why shouldn't I understand?" Kazanov replied. And added, "A fine hand. Meticulous letters."

"So he has pretty handwriting," Devorah interjected. "How do you know he'll teach the children to write like that?"

Kazanov ignored her comment and asked the tutor, "Do you have any students yet?"

Itzkowitz felt that everything depended on this crucial question. He answered hesitantly, "Well, of course there are. I've been promised . . ."

2. The phrase comes from one of the fables by Krylov, called "The Dragonfly and the Ant." These are the first two words of the fable in the Russian and mean "dragonfly" and "ant."

"Who's sending you their children?"

"Sending, well, nobody's sent me any yet. But I've been promised."

"Now do you understand?" Devorah gave her husband a look. "Nobody is sending their children yet. You'd be the first to jump in. They'll tar and feather you."

"With all due respect, ma'am," Itzkowitz turned to her with a pleading voice, "you have to understand that if everyone said this, nothing would ever be accomplished. Somebody has to be the first."

"He's quite right," Kazanov agreed.

"Listen, Reb Mendel," the tutor said passionately, "I can see that you're putting yourself in my shoes. Let me speak frankly. You understand, don't you, how important it is for someone to go first. So, if you're the first, I'll make it cheaper—a lot cheaper—for you than for the others. Of course, this would stay between us. Usually, my fee is a ruble a month per student . . ."

"A ruble a month! That means for two girls it's twelve rubles a semester! Do you hear this, you madman?" Devorah cried.

"Shush, let the man have his say," her husband stopped her.

"Please, ma'am," Itzkowitz said softly. "I'm a person, too. You can see that, can't you? I, too, have to eat and drink. How many students can I have? Well, let's figure ten or, tops, twelve. If I charge less than a ruble, how will I make a living? But with you, I'll make a different deal. Little girl, leave us alone here for a moment," he said to the girl who'd been standing there absorbing every word of the discussion.

Obediently, the girl walked away.

"Listen," he said in a low voice. "I'll take seventy-five kopecks a month for both girls, but you have to tell everyone you're paying two rubles a month."

"Well, what else can you ask for?" Kazanov said, looking at his wife and holding up his hands.

His wife was forced to capitulate. "Of course, seventy-five kopecks a month isn't big money . . . but still, it's something . . ."

"Well, there's nothing to talk about anymore. It's decided! I'm giving him the children to teach. Good luck!" the man finally concluded, and he shook hands with Itzkowitz.

"Father!" the girl who'd returned unnoticed cried out rapturously. She threw herself on her father's neck.

"Shh, shh, don't get so excited," her mother stopped her. "Studying isn't as easy as you think. You'll get tapped on the knuckles with the ruler so much they'll ache. I know; I've seen what tutors do. What, isn't that true?" she said to Itzkowitz.

"Naturally," the tutor responded, smiling, "if you act up and don't write well, you'll get it on the knuckles."

"I won't act up."

"In fact, I'm asking you to be even stricter with them," the mother told the tutor. "If they don't behave, you're even allowed to smack them, yes, indeed."

"Only when they really act up," Itzkowitz agreed. "Sticks are probably cheap here, yes?"

But these words made little impression on the girl, and she ran to share the good news with her sister.

"My dear, well-behaved children," the father praised them, "you'll enjoy teaching them . . . Well, come into the house; we'll drink to it."

A bit tipsy from the two shots of liquor, Itzkowitz returned home for supper and announced, "Well, ma'am, you can congratulate me."

"What," Chana Leah asked in a satisfied tone, "do you have a lot of students already?"

"A lot, well, not a lot, but things are beginning to move. You'll see, I will have students!"

"Of course," Chana Leah agreed. "You can't imagine how the town is bubbling. Every single person is insisting that these days you have to send children to study. And I'll tell you a secret: you've made a good impression on everyone here."

After supper Itzkowitz ventured into town again, but this time he had less success. In one house they simply said no, in the other he found no one home, and they banished him from the third. Of the six houses he went to, only one garnered him a promise that "we'll think about it." His mood turned glum again. All day he'd been walking around. He'd gone to the richest householders, and all he'd gotten was one lesson at seventy-five a month total. It appeared he wouldn't actually manage to earn enough in this place, and he'd be compelled to return to Vitebsk and starve as before.

It had already grown dark. Itzkowitz walked about lost in thought, a dejected expression on his face. Suddenly, he heard someone calling him: "Teacher. Stop for a moment."

Across the street in the window of a large house, he saw a girl about nineteen years old with a round freckled face and blonde wavy hair, wearing a red ribbon around her neck. The girl was clearly uneasy; she looked around anxiously. But there was no one on the street except Itzkowitz.

"Come inside. Nobody's here. I must tell you something," she said in a voice trembling with excitement.

Itzkowitz went into the house.

"Do you already have a lot of girls who want to study with you?" was the question she greeted him with.

"I have . . . several."

"Who exactly?"

"Mendel Kazanov is sending me his two girls, Zalmen Isser . . ."

"*Those* people!" the girl cried scornfully. "Why didn't you come to us? Do you know who my father is? Leivik Yachnes, the timber merchant. You've probably heard of him."

"Yes, I have. Of course!" Itzkowitz found it necessary to agree.

"You should have come to us before anyone else. What are you going to teach?"

"Reading, writing."

"In Russian? I know Russian already. I copy it out of a handwriting textbook. Can you also teach German?"

"Whatever you want," Itzkowitz answered confidently. All he knew was the German alphabet.

"By all means, try. Write in German: Esther Dvoshe Burakovic."

Itzkowitz sat down at the table and wrote what she asked.

Esther Dvoshe began to copy what he'd written. Pointing at each letter, she asked confidently, "Good? Good?"

"Very good."

"Yes! Now write 'Miloslavka' in German."

This word, too, she copied out, then hid the paper from which she'd copied the word. After that, they began to hammer out an agreement.

"The price depends on whether you want a private lesson or together with others."

"Private, private," she cried impetuously. "I have no intention of sitting alongside bratty girls."

"If it's private and for an entire hour, it's . . . two rubles," Itzkowitz said hesitantly.

Esther Dvoshe burst into loud laughter and offered fifty kopecks, then seventy-five. They agreed on one ruble, half of which the student would have to pay secretly so that her mother wouldn't find out.

As Itzkowitz made ready to leave, Esther Dvoshe, in a show of bravado, stretched out her hand to him.[3] "If you think we're all old-fashioned Jews here," she said coquettishly, "you're mistaken . . . See, I'm not afraid to shake hands with a man."

"I'm not old-fashioned, either," the tutor replied breathlessly.

"You'll see," Esther Dvoshe said with an air of excitement, "you'll see . . . Sometimes people even go secretly on strolls. When nobody's looking. Yes! Here in Miloslavka, there are also modern people." And she threw the tutor a passionate look.

---

3. Devout Jews refrain from physical contact between the sexes. Esther is flaunting her renouncing of tradition by stretching out her hand for Itzkowitz to shake.

When he left, Itzkowitz walked around for several minutes as if he were drunk, still feeling the touch of the girl's hand on his own.

"Hold it. That's you, the writing tutor!" an elderly man sitting in a shop yelled from across the street.

Nervously, Itzkowitz turned to see who was calling out to him, and, when he saw the man, he immediately answered, "Yes, yes. It's me."

"A fine occupation you have. Couldn't you find anything better to do?"

Itzkowitz, figuring that this was an opening to a conversation about his lessons, replied tensely, "It's a job, like any other job. A person has to make a living."

"What, are you dying of hunger?"

"Maybe, just maybe, I am dying of hunger. How would you know? And why is it any of your business?" Itzkowitz answered, then stalked away.

"You're not only a goy, you're an audacious one at that. May you be taken away by a horrible death," the shopkeeper yelled after him.

The next morning Itzkowitz had two happy surprises. As soon as he finished his prayers, a girl ran breathlessly into the room and burst out, "Mother said you should come to us."

"Who's your mother? Whose daughter are you?"

"You were at our house just yesterday. My mother is Tzirel, the wife of Menachem Treines of Dubrov."

The tutor recalled that this was the same little girl he'd found sleeping on the sofa in the house where the woman had so rudely sent him off.

"Very well, little girl. Tell your mother I'll come soon. Do you know why she's calling me?" he added.

"Mother wants to send us to you to study," the girl replied. "She says, 'these days . . . ' We're all going to study—me, my sister Rivka'le, and my cousin Gnendele. Poor thing, she's a penniless orphan and stays with us for free. My father is very rich, he's the richest man in town, and we'll pay more than everyone else."

As soon as the girl left the house, Chana Leah cried out, "Well! What did I tell you? Ah, I'm kvelling. The old sow found out that others were sending their children to study, so she got scared. Didn't want her kids to be the last ones. Let me tell you, don't give her a cheap price. It's okay, she won't get sick if she pays an extra ruble a month. Naturally, she'll haggle, but don't lower your rate. Don't worry, she'll pay more just so no one can say she can't afford to send her kids to study."

A little later another messenger came by, a boy about twelve years old, wearing a long jacket and an astrakhan hat. "The melamed said you should come to the cheder right now," he said in a bold tone, gazing mockingly right into the tutor's eyes.

"Who's your melamed?"

"Rachel's husband, Reb Yosel. Our cheder is near the old synagogue. He said you should come immediately."

"Why does he need me?" Itzkowitz wondered.

"He'll tell you that himself," the boy answered brazenly, and added, "I have to go study now. The lesson is starting."

Chana Leah thought for a while. "Ay, ay," she suddenly figured it out. "This boy is the son of Gedalia and Mirel. Gedalia works for a wealthy timber merchant and is constantly in Russia. He probably told his wife that the children should study Russian."

9

Itzkowitz left the house, cheerful and confident. But his first encounter wasn't at all a happy one. An old, stooped lady with a thick prayer book under her arm crossed his path. Spotting him, she stopped, glared at him angrily, and spoke in a low voice, rapidly and expressively as when one mumbles the special chant to ward off an evil eye. "Go to hell, you lecher, you heretic and convert. What demon brought you here? May you break your loins, neck, hands, and feet. Lord of the universe: at least for the sake of my poor orphans, strike him down in defeat. *Tfu, tfu, tfu.*"[1]

And she quickly walked away.

Itzkowitz remained standing there, astounded, alarmed by this unexpected attack. So much pain and contempt were palpable in the old woman's curses; he understood immediately that they arose from something more than mere religious fanaticism.

"Who's that old woman?" he asked a passing boy.

---

1. Sound of spitting. Spitting three times in reaction to something very good or very bad is an old Jewish superstition.

"Bluma the Yiddish teacher."

Now Itzkowitz understood why she'd cursed him. He was robbing her of her daily bread.

In the cheder, Itzkowitz found Yosel, the melamed, giving a Hebrew lesson to the boys. He was a young man with a small blond beard, slightly squinty eyes, and thin, tight lips. Four boys sat around the table.

Yosel rose slightly from his chair, shook Itzkowitz's hand, invited him to sit down, and immediately got to the point: the father of one of his students was currently in the Russian heartland and wanted his boys to learn Russian. Since there were no tutors in town, he—Yosel—who knew a bit of Russian, had to undertake the job of teaching them. But the father was now demanding that the children should write him short letters in Russian, and this was something Yosel could not teach them. He himself barely knew more than the alphabet. Now that a tutor had arrived, however, the mother of the boys had asked Yosel to discuss with him the possibility of teaching the children.

Yosel related all of this in a calm, unemotional tone; cold, as if talking about something he couldn't care less about. "I'd be very happy if you could free me of this duty and teach them Russian. This is no job for me."

Itzkowitz agreed that teaching Russian was no job for a melamed. To teach Russian, one had to be a specialist. He began to ask about money, but Yosel responded dryly that Itzkowitz would have to talk to the mother of the children regarding his compensation.

"Fine," Itzkowitz agreed and left right away.

Yosel followed him out. In the vestibule he stopped and whispered in his ear. "The children were watching me, so I couldn't talk to you the way I wished. It's not fitting, you know, for a melamed to get involved in this sort of business. But speaking bluntly, I very much want you to accept the teaching position. This way, I'd also be able to sneak in and learn something . . . but we can talk about that another time. Listen, go to the boys' mother and ask her to talk to the mothers of the other boys. She'll do it if you agree to only charge her fifty kopecks. I'll throw in a good word, too. I'll say that I'll be at the private lessons. Understand? That way, they won't be afraid, you know, of a corrupting influence . . . as usual. Understand?"

"I understand, I understand. Thank you very much."

Yosel was quiet for a while and after a moment of hesitation, blurted out, "There's a young man who wants to meet you . . . he lives here in the courtyard. He has some sort of business for you. Of course, no one is to know about this . . . Go in through this door. He's there, alone in the room. He's waiting for you."

"Who is he?"

"Melech, Akiva's son. He's engaged to be married."

"Does he want to study?"

"Who knows? To study, not to study . . . talk to him and you'll find out. But this should stay between us. Well, I wish you luck." And he quickly returned to the classroom.

Itzkowitz stepped through the door Yosel had indicated and encountered a hunchbacked young man with a dull complexion and frightened eyes. "Come in. Come," the man said quickly to the tutor, pointing to the room next door. "No one's in there."

Once they were there, he whispered, "I beg of you, can you write letters in Russian?"

"Yes," Itzkowitz answered, somewhat confused by the question.

"All different kinds of letters?"

"Yes, different kinds."

"Even to a fiancée?"

"Yes, even to a fiancée."

"And you're probably able to read different sorts of letters, too. I mean, all kinds of handwriting?"

"Yes, sure I can."

"Listen . . ."

The young man told Itzkowitz his predicament. Two months ago he'd become engaged to a girl from Minsk, a very educated girl. The matchmaker had naturally duped her into believing that the groom was also educated, that he was knowledgeable in the "seven wisdoms of the world," and fluent in nearly all seventy languages. Now his fiancée had written a Russian letter to him and requested that he respond entirely in Russian. He had appealed to Yosel, but Yosel couldn't read the letter, either.

"So now you understand," he concluded in a businesslike tone. "This is the kind of thing that can break an engagement, something this stupid."

"So you want to learn how to write a Russian letter—" Itzkowitz began.

"No, no," he quickly interrupted him. "Why should I study? I don't have the time or need for it. I'm getting married. That's just what I need, to go and study now."

"Well, then, what do you want?"

"Quite simple: I want you to write the letter for me. So far, I've received two letters from her in Russian. So you'll read them to me now and translate. Afterwards, you'll take a small piece of paper and write down what I tell you. I'll say it in Yiddish and you'll write it in Russian. Obviously, you should add a few, you know, stylistic flourishes; that's very important. And also, address the envelope."

Itzkowitz thought for a while, then shook his head and replied, "This is a very difficult matter."

"Why is it difficult? If you know how to write, it can't be that difficult for you. Anyway, to cut to the chase, how much do you want?"

"Per letter?"

"No, by the month! I don't want to do it by the letter. I want to hire you for the month, and you'll write as many letters as I need. The most important thing is that as soon as I get a letter, you read it to me immediately and write a response."

"For work like this, I can't take less than three rubles a month," Itzkowitz replied decisively.

The young man clutched his head in shock. He explained to Itzkowitz that he won't take up that much of his time and that it wasn't right of Itzkowitz to take advantage of another person's need, especially because he'd have to pay without his father's knowledge. Itzkowitz deducted a ruble from the fee, and the deal was sealed for two rubles a month. They decided that in the evening, after Yosel's lesson in the cheder was over, Itzkowitz would cautiously sneak in to meet with Melech, unobserved.

Itzkowitz left to go to the home of Tzirel, Men-achem Treines's wife. This time, the matron greeted him much more affably.

"Have a seat. Why did you run away so quickly yesterday?" she reproached him as if she were the offended one. "Of course, I was angry that Chana Leah had bothered me without consulting me. But I have nothing against *you*. Has anyone given you their children yet?"

Itzkowitz listed all the householders who were either sending him or had promised to send him their kids.

"If I send you my girls, then all the others will send you theirs," Tzirel assured him. "But upon my word, I don't know what to do. After all, they go to the teacher."

"I teach both Yiddish and Russian, and you can be certain I know Yiddish better than the girls' teacher."

"No, let them learn Yiddish from the teacher, poor old lady. She's already been here and cried me a river of tears. I have a gentle heart. Another thirty kopecks a month is no great misfortune. Thank God, it's not a large sum for me, I can afford it. Besides, if you don't teach the children Yiddish, you'll charge me less. How much do you charge? I have two daughters, may they be healthy, and a niece, an orphan. And a neighbor also asked me to let her daughter study with mine."

After much haggling, they settled on two rubles and fifty kopecks.

"I know I could have bargained it down another fifty kopecks," Tzirel said, "but I don't want to. I'd rather pay fifty kopecks more, because then you'll teach the children better. These aren't ordinary children, you know. They're not just Zalmen Isser's children."

By now, Itzkowitz had arranged for seven rubles' worth of private lessons. Whichever way you looked at it, this was a substantial base. And there would definitely be another five rubles' worth coming.

That day and the next, Itzkowitz continued his visits. Now when he came into someone's home, he no longer found it necessary to vouch for himself but instead went directly to the point, explaining that he already had many students, that he charged very little and taught very well, and at the end he'd always add, "I heard that your little girl, may she be healthy, has a good head. In two months' time, I'll teach her writing, reading, and math so well that the entire town will be buzzing about her."

The result of these three days of feverish bustling was stellar. Itzkowitz acquired eighteen students for a total of ten rubles and fifty kopecks. He hadn't expected such a tremendous sum. Ten-and-a-half rubles! This was a fortune. And he wasn't even done yet. Two or three women who'd promised to mull it over would surely decide to send him their children, and then—then he would have as good as twelve or thirteen rubles a month!

The only thing spoiling his good mood was his doubt over whether some of the families would actually pay him. When Itzkowitz had recited the names of the families to Chana Leah, she'd scowled acutely at two of the names. "Leib's wife, Shifra? Zalmen Isser's wife?" she'd drawled unhappily. "Oy, I don't like them at all."

"Why?" he winced.

"It's forbidden to speak badly of others, but I'm afraid they won't pay up."

"Why?"

"Because they made some bad business deals recently, especially Shifra. They don't even own the hair on their heads! I'm sure she deliberately signed up her girls so people would think she's well-to-do. . . . Hmm, though it's just possible she'll pay you because she won't want to humiliate herself."

That same evening, Itzkowitz arranged for his food and lodging. He was pleased with the attic room at Chana Leah's. He was also satisfied with the food. In the middle of his haggling over the price with Chana Leah, she stopped abruptly and said, "You know what, let it be seven rubles, as you wish. But you'll have to teach my granddaughter. She keeps pestering me: all the girls are going to study and she isn't. She won't take any extra time. Just squeeze her in with the other children, no matter where. She's a good girl. She'll behave."

The tutor agreed to this, especially because Chana Leah hadn't asked for the reward he'd promised her for her "help."

10

For days, Itzkowitz was the most popular man in town. Everywhere—in the market, in the synagogue, in people's homes—all anyone spoke about was the tutor. Reports about each word he uttered, each gesture he made, spread immediately around the entire town and became the topic of endless discussions. But while women, both the young and the old, spoke openly in their homes, shops, and on the streets about the "unheard-of event," the men, especially the melamdim, the Hebrew school teachers, as well as other religious functionaries—the cantor, the ritual slaughterer, and the scribe—spoke about Itzkowitz reluctantly. It was beneath their dignity and status to show interest in such trivial matters.

If a businessman or householder approached a melamed or slaughterer, asking, "Have you seen our newest visitor yet? The jewel?" the other would put on an innocent expression, "Which visitor? Which jewel?"

"What do you mean, which visitor? Haven't you heard? The tutor! The writer! The whole town is topsy-turvy."

"To hell with him! So, he came here. He can be my grandmother's problem. What do I care if he breaks his neck!"

"Mark my words, soon he'll bring apostasy, subversive books, into this town," the man warned.

The melamed would give him a scornful smile and answer calmly, "Well, let's just assume he won't have any luck spreading apostasy. It'll never take hold. Miloslavka isn't Vilna, thank God."

But his calm and confidence were only external, a pretense. When they were alone, the melamdim and other pious Jews talked about the tutor with much more anxiety.

"Did you hear? What do you think?" one melamed would ask the other as soon as they met.

"It's a disaster. A disaster!" the other, also upset, replied.

"It can't be allowed. We should do something."

"Not should. *Must!*" the second amended.

And they'd quickly go their separate ways.

On the fourth day after the tutor's arrival, when he'd already lined up all his students for his lessons, a few melamdim and some other pious Jews gathered in the synagogue after morning prayers. The gathering hadn't been planned, but everyone expected that a conversation about the tutor would soon start up. Each one waited for the other to start.

One of the melamdim, a tall man with an angry, dirt colored face and a black beard starting to grey, wrapped up his tefillin quickly and nervously, and with lowered eyes, as if he were talking to himself, he muttered, "They're saying he even got himself a job in a cheder." He shrugged.

"This town has gone insane," another melamed added, also shrugging.

"Where did he come from? What devil brought him here?" a third one cried furiously, resentfully.

"Where did he come from? Vilna, where else!" another said.

A short, plump, well-dressed young man with a protruding belly, a wide pale face overgrown with a black beard, and an audacious expression on his face, went over to the group. As he slowly removed his tallis, his prayer shawl adorned with a silver neckband, he said confidently and decisively, "But I've always said, haven't I, that Miloslavka is a free-for-all? Who ever heard of a thing like this? Who ever saw a thing like this? Any sort of rat or scoundrel moves into a town and does whatever he pleases! Think about it. A writer comes prancing into town, opens a secular school—and nothing! Everyone pretends not to notice. It's nothing less than Sodom!"

"Isser is right," they all agreed.

"What's going on?" Isser continued. "Where are the respectable men? Where are the people? Where's the town? The first day this scoundrel got here, we should have kicked him out and taught him such a lesson, he wouldn't have dared try it again."

"Isser, I see you've forgotten that we're Jews; we're in exile," said the scribe, a little old man with gloomy eyes and a face like parchment. "It's easy to say, 'kick him out.' How're you going to do that? What can you do to him? Ay, ay."

"Bah! It's not that hard. We just have to get moving on it," Isser replied. "All we have to do is take a pound of tea and a few rubles to the district police officer, and tomorrow the scoundrel will be gone."

"The district police officer. . . . A pound of tea," an elderly man said, tilting his head skeptically. "You forget that you're dealing with a 'writer.' Start with him, and he'll make trouble for the whole town. I see you're not familiar with that breed. You can be sure this apostate will cozy up to the police officer faster than we will."

"Forget about going to the police officer! We can get rid of him another way," Isser said. "Let's grab him on a quiet little street somewhere and break his bones. No one will see or hear a thing. It's the best method for a scoundrel like him. We give him this kind of treatment, and he'll run off to where peppers grow."

"That's not the Jewish way. It's not a Jewish strategy," the elderly scribe protested, shaking his head.

"Isser, you're forgetting one small thing," said an old rheumy-eyed man, shaking his head back and forth. "You're forgetting that to beat someone up, you need strength, vigor. Do we have any strong men? You can be sure he's stronger than all of us put together. None of us eat pork, right? And he's probably eaten many pounds of pork already. So what can be done to him?"

"In my opinion," a tall melamed said, "and I'm saying this quite frankly, everything depends on Rabbi Chaim'ke. He's the rabbi. He runs the town; he's lord of the manor. If he would've wanted it, this scoundrel would've been gone a long time ago. Yes, I'm not afraid to say it. Rabbi Chaim'ke is a fine, sincere Jew—truly!—but other than his holy texts, he's not interested in anything, and he doesn't do anything. . . . Yesterday we went to him and told him that some sort of writer had come to town. We told him this writer could do harm, may God protect us. And what did he do? Nothing! He moaned, he sighed, he said that Jews are in exile, and that's it."

"Shush. What chutzpah you have to talk that way about Rabbi Chaim'ke," Isser shouted angrily. "All of us together aren't worth his little toe. I also went to talk to him. He nearly burst into tears; he's crushed, but what can he do about it?"

"What do you mean, what?" one teacher cried out. "He's the rabbi. He can command. He can command even Ashmedai himself. And you're telling me he couldn't at least call a meeting?"

"Quiet!" Isser cut in. "You don't know what you're talking about. Command, you say! You forget that these days, Rabbi Chaim'ke isn't exactly in the position to command anyone. You know perfectly well he hasn't been paid wages for the last six months and a lot of the important people in this town aren't all that satisfied with him. At least if he knew he had the people on his side . . . But you can see for yourself: the apostate just barely shows up here and already everyone has sent him their children."

"It's the women," someone threw in.

"The women do nothing without the men."

"Why point fingers at the women? Why at the men? The melamdim themselves are friends with him and send him their students!" said a young man, the scribe's son, and he glanced at Yosel, who'd been standing quietly the entire time.

Yosel, unnerved by this unexpected reproach, timidly walked over to the group and spoke in a bitter tone. "You're criticizing me, Shmerel, but it's easy for you to talk. You all know the position I was in. 'Do not judge your fellow man until you have been in his place.'[1] Gedalia's wife, Mirel, pressured me into teaching her children Russian. What would you have done? You'd just antagonize the parents of your students? And what, have no way of making a living? I'm asking you all. Is it my fault that Gedalia is pigheaded and insisted his children learn Russian? Do you think I'm happy about this writer coming here? If anyone thinks so, say it openly."

These remarks had them all flummoxed. To bring the argument to a close, Isser declared, "No, obviously no one's blaming you, Yosel. You're not at fault; it's Gedalia. The devil only knows what's happened to him since he went to the Russian heartland."

"Listen," the melamed with the angry face spoke up again. "Let's not talk about who's to blame. We're all to blame! But now we have to do something about it. We can't just leave things as they are. I'm convinced the tutor didn't just decide to come here on his own. The Vilna group is behind this. They must have sent him. That's how they operate. The problem isn't studying Russian; many pious Jews know how to read

---

1. *Pirkei Avot* (Ethics of the Fathers) 2:5

and write Russian. No, it's the Jewishness part. Do you get it? The Jew-ish-ness! The Vilna group is cautious. They don't come out in the open; they work stealthily. They have those secular books that say terrible things. If this heretic tutor settles here, he'll spread his contagious disease everywhere: in the cheder, among the youth. He'll utter a word to this one, give a book to that one, then he'll lead two or three boys down the wrong path, and there, that'll be the end of it! It'll start a fire we won't be able to extinguish. We must tear this disease out by its roots immediately. Today. We can't wait even a single day!"

The melamed's vehement words made a deep impression on everyone. They all grew quiet, pondering.

Gershon the beadle, who'd been listening attentively to the conversation, now joined in: "Forgive me for having the audacity to intrude on your discussion," he said humbly, but with inner confidence. "You're saying all kinds of things about this tutor. That he's from *that* group, that he's a troublemaker, an apostate . . . Forgive me, but I believe you're mistaken. It's true I'm not a great scholar, but I do have eyes. Three days ago the tutor was here for afternoon prayers. Afterwards, he stayed for two hours and studied the Gemara aloud. I listened, and in my opinion, he's not a troublemaker. He studied with such passion and such sweetness, and chanted with such a lovely melody. Say what you want. Someone who eats pork couldn't do this."

"Oh, oh, you hear, you hear, he pores over the Gemara!" the angry teacher said. "Do you even know what this means? Do you know that the most ardent freethinkers, especially the heretics, also pore over the

Gemara? They study it specially, so they'll know how to be heretics."

"But the passion, the sweetness," Gershon tried again.

"Listen to me," said an old man who'd been sitting a little ways away during the entire conversation. "You have to look at everything from all angles. I figure Menachem is right. We have to pull the evil out by its roots. And immediately! But we have to know how to do it. Before we do anything, let's take a close look at this character. I've seen him on the street, too. It's true, he dresses like a freethinker, but he looks quite decent. Believe me, I have a sixth sense for these things. In my opinion, we should use *midas harachmim*, mercy, before we use *midas hadin* and judge him with the full rigor of the law. We're Jews. We're obliged to be merciful. And who knows, maybe there's still a Jewish spark in him and it's still possible to get him to repent."

"True, true," the scribe agreed and sighed deeply.

"Who will talk to him?"

"Let Yosel talk to him," the scribe's son said, with a spiteful smile.

"Go to hell! Let the Angel of Death talk to him!" Yosel cried.

"Shush, why're you getting so angry?" the old man said, trying to calm Yosel down. "Actually, it *should* be you. You'll see him every day. So you can watch him, start a conversation about a topic in the Gemara, scrutinize him, dig around a bit to figure him out. Slowly, you'll start guiding him in the right direction with questions like: What's the purpose of things? What's their meaning? You're not stupid. You'll know what to say."

"Let Isser talk to him, instead," Yosel suggested.

"It won't hurt if both of you do."

"I'm willing," Isser said, laughing. "Of course, I'll try talking to him nicely. If I succeed, fine. If not, I won't be embarrassed to give him a few slaps. I know how to act tough."

They all burst into laughter.

"Don't be so quick with your smacks," the good-natured old man said. "Slapping a person isn't such a smart thing to do. First, try to light the Jewish spark in him. That's what's most important."

"You're playing with fire, I'm telling you," the angry Hebrew teacher said. "I say we don't need to look for any Jewish spark in him. While you're looking for his 'Jewish spark,' he'll sow hundreds of sparks of heresy that'll light a hellfire. Anyway, do whatever you want." And he stalked off furiously.

11

By Friday of his first week in Miloslavka, Itzkowitz had finalized the arrangements for his private lessons and decided to start working on Sunday.

Of course, he had no pedagogical plan at all. Not only had he never taught children before, but he'd never even observed others teaching. His only acquaintance with the field was the one method used by the Vitebsk freethinker who'd taught him Russian, which he was convinced was the only possible approach. In general, he assumed teaching to be effortless and uncomplicated: teach students the alphabet, show them how to put syllables together, compel them to learn by heart, and assign them writing exercises, copying words from handwriting models or straight out of books.

As for his personal knowledge and expertise, Itzkowitz worried even less. He could write Yiddish and Russian in a neat, precise script. He knew the German alphabet. He was able to read a simple Russian book—not too fluently, true, but without stumbling. He could recite ten Krylov fables by heart. He knew grammar, at least the verbs, almost without errors, and the four operations of arithmetic. These skills seemed so prodigious to him that he was certain his students would take years to learn them.

Despite his confidence, he could not rid himself of a certain sense of unease. Teaching children to read and write was no great feat, yet families would be paying him real money—actual rubles and half-rubles!—and what would he be giving them in return? Though Itzkowitz always argued that in these modern times one had to study, and tried constantly to convince himself that education was extremely important, deep down he considered education a frivolous, worthless thing that was easy to do without. It seemed crazy to him that serious-minded, thoughtful householders were willing to pay actual money for his work. That's why a teacher's position appeared to him unstable, tenuous.

As he set about organizing his lesson schedule, Itzkowitz leafed through his textbooks. He skimmed several pages of the reader, glanced into the grammar and arithmetic texts; reassured, he put them away. He was so certain there'd never be the need to teach higher-level studies in this town, he didn't even bother opening the history and geography texts. Despite never having read these books, the fact that he possessed them made him feel that he already knew the material. And were anyone to ask him whether he knew history or geography, he would reply quite sincerely, "What do you mean, do I know history and geography? They're not such simple subjects, the kind you can master completely. They're vast. But I do know a lot. I mean, I know the main parts: the beginning and the end. I even have history and geography books that contain everything, from beginning to end."

Over the course of the last few days, Itzkowitz managed with various pretexts to avoid going to the synagogue. But on Friday night he went along with Leivik, the innkeeper.

In the synagogue, the worshippers didn't take their eyes off him. From every direction, he was met with fierce, sarcastic, or at best, curious glances. A few young boys stuck by his side during the entire prayer service. They stood staring obnoxiously at him, their mouths hanging open, as one stares at a wild animal. One of them even reached out to touch him, as if to convince himself that this wasn't a mirage but a real live person.

Right before the reading of the Torah, Isser—the young man who'd taken part in the discussion with the other melamdim—came over to Itzkowitz. Earnest, smug, nose in the air, he nonchalantly tossed his tallis over his shoulders, ambled over to the tutor, and in the manner of a confident householder, asked loudly, "So, you're the tutor?"

Itzkowitz startled at this sudden question. He turned quickly, and at the sight of the well-dressed man, he replied hastily, flustered, "Yes, that's me."

"Where are you from?"

"From Vitebsk."

"Are you planning to stay?"

"I think so . . . I don't know . . . I'll see."

Itzkowitz was offended both by the questioner's severe tone and by the way he addressed Itzkowitz with the less respectful "du." But because he didn't know who the man was and the silver neckband on the man's tallis impressed him, he decided to answer humbly and respectfully.

Isser, in turn, was very pleased by the tutor's humility and respect, and he continued speaking in the same tone as before. "Couldn't you find another trade?"

"What a question!" Itzkowitz answered diffidently. "If I'd found another type of work, of course I wouldn't have bothered with this one."

This answer pleased Isser even more. *No, he isn't a scoundrel*, he thought. *It's possible to talk to him.* He sat down next to Itzkowitz and asked him softly, "How many lessons' worth do you have already?"

"Well, I'm still far from becoming a rich man."

"But how many?"

"Eight rubles' worth," Itzkowitz answered, deliberately concealing his actual earnings.

"Pitiful, very pitiful," Isser said with a bit of empathy. "Eight rubles! That's not much money. I mean, if you're going to eat pork, at least let its juices run down your beard. Make up your mind! Either this or that. If not, how does any of this make sense? Where does it lead to? What's the point? Right?"

"Definitely," Itzkowitz said, smiling.

Isser was silent for a while. Then he asked, "I heard you're a bit of a Torah scholar?"

"A bit."

"Tell me the truth. Don't you miss the Gemara? And Jewish life?"

"What does it matter if I *do* miss it?" Itzkowitz answered with a sigh. "You know the saying: 'If you can't jump over it, you have to slide under it.'"

Isser agreed that this was true. He decided: *Okay, that's enough for the first time.* Adjusting his tallis on his shoulders, he said affably, "Since that's the case, since you're a bit of a Gemara scholar, we should talk. I'll invite you over for tea one day."

He strutted back to his spot as proudly as he'd left it, coquettishly letting his tallis drag across the floor, like a triumphant rooster trailing its majestic plumage.

12

After a heavy, greasy, filling Shabbos afternoon meal, after Leivik and Chana Leah had lain down to nap, Itzkowitz went into his room and secretly smoked a cigarette.[1] He sat in front of the oven, blowing the cigarette smoke into it, and as he did so, he began to reminisce about his not-too-distant past. His life had been full of hunger and cold, he'd never eaten as filling a meal as this one, yet how happily and pleasantly he used to spend the Shabbos day. Each week a group of Maskilim would gather in the shared quarters where he lived, along with several other boys who'd also been cast out of the defunct yeshiva. They would have interesting conversations, read books, debate complex theological questions, make plans for the future. All of them were preoccupied with progress, with education. Their souls felt airy, optimistic. Life was bright; they believed in life, in a future. And here? How dark

1. Smoking a cigarette is a violation of Shabbos law, as it entails the lighting of a fire, which is the second of the thirty-nine categories of ritual work forbidden on Shabbos.

everything had become! Snuffed out! Not a single person he felt close to, not one lively conversation. Alone, lonely, in a dense forest . . .

Itzkowitz smoked the cigarette down to its butt, painstakingly dispersed it among the ashes, and sighed deeply. He paced back and forth across the room, then paused in front of the small window that looked out on the quiet little street. Only a few huts, spaced widely apart, were scattered along the street. Beyond the street lay orchards, and beyond the orchards, thick, shadowy woods. The street was dead and barren. But at one hut, a young man in a long overcoat and cloth hat stood leaning firmly against a wall, staring continuously in the direction of Leivik's inn, as if he were waiting for something.

For a few minutes, the young man stood still, but then he began to pace up and down the street. Soon, Sara'ke, Leivik's grandchild, came out of the inn. The young man stopped her and spoke to her. In response, the little girl pointed toward Itzkowitz's attic room. When the girl left, the young man looked around cautiously and quickly stepped into the inn.

Itzkowitz, who had been closely observing the exchange, understood instinctively that he'd been the subject of the young man's question to Sara'ke. He felt uneasy. What could this stranger want? Had someone sent him to nose around, to see what Itzkowitz was up to? Had the young man perhaps noticed the cigarette smoke?

He moved away from the window and listened to the cautious footsteps on the stairs. Soon he heard soft knocking at the door.

"Who's there?" he asked loudly, anxiously.

The door opened and the young man he'd seen came into the room. His mouth was open and he had barely sprouting whiskers and light blue, naïve, honest eyes. His complexion, reddened by excitement, shone with inner passion.

"It's me," he said in a quavering tone, looking about him with a confused smile. "I snuck in here so that no one would notice me. I want . . . I have to talk to you about something . . . I, I'm a Maskil!" he whispered with fervor.

"Shush. Quiet." Frightened, Itzkowitz stopped him and looked around. "Who are you?"

"I'm Elya, Shmuel and Chaya's son. My father owns the tavern and is a bread merchant. You saw me in the synagogue. . . . I mean, I saw you."

Itzkowitz opened the door and peeked out, scanning the attic. Reassured that no one was within earshot, he said in a more relaxed tone, "So, what do you want? What is it you want to say?"

"The first thing I want to tell you," Elya replied in a serious, nearly elegiac tone, "is to be careful! You can't imagine how furious the pious Jews are. You wouldn't believe the things they're saying! Yesterday I heard them talking about you, and I trembled."

"What did they say?" Itzkowitz asked, nervousness in his voice.

"Do you really want to know what they said? Everything! Everything you can imagine. That you're from Vilna, that you're a dangerous heretic, that some kind of 'group' sent you here to lead the whole town astray. Terrible things, terrible!"

"It's not true," Itzkowitz said, turning pale. "I'm nothing—"

"Wait, listen to this," Elya interrupted, "Do you know who stuck up for you? You're not going to believe it. The beadle! He promised everyone you were studying fervently in the synagogue all night. Ha-ha!" Elya laughed happily.

Itzkowitz was relieved. Already, he felt like explaining to this young man, this kindred spirit, that he'd done it on purpose. But he reminded himself that, in fact, he didn't know this person at all and couldn't be sure if he was trustworthy.

"Listen to me," Itzkowitz said. "I don't know you and so I can't be frank with you. If you want me to believe that you're a Maskil, smoke a cigarette now."

"Smoke a cigarette?" Elya was stunned by the unexpected request, but soon he caught on and smiled broadly. "Why not?" he cried. "I don't actually smoke, but to show you that I'm a freethinker, I'll do it. I'll even eat pork." Smiling, he took a cigarette from Itzkowitz and smoked it ineptly. He drew two puffs and asked triumphantly, "Well, do you believe me now?"

"Yes, now I see you're one of us," Itzkowitz replied earnestly, and after taking a drag on the cigarette, he quashed it and somewhat solemnly said, "Well, then, listen. You should know that I'm one of the authentic ones, one of the real Maskilim! My studying the Gemara was only for the sake of appearances."

"Certainly, certainly. I understand. I get it completely," Elya said, impressed. "And they thought you were really studying. So, do you know what they decided to do? You won't believe it! They intend to bring you back to the correct path, to prevail upon you to abandon your secular studies and sit down with the Gemara instead. Hahaha!"

"No matter how long they torment themselves, they won't have any effect on me! But this is good. It's very good," Itzkowitz said.

"Of course, it's good."

"I'll be leading them around by their noses; I'll fool them however I can."

"Of course, of course. Do you know that when Ezriel's son, Isser, came over to you today, that was the beginning of it. Otherwise, he'd—naturally—never approach you. I know him quite well."

"Really? Those cunning beasts! Well, I'm no fool, either."

"But you have to be on guard!"

"Don't worry about me. I'll know how to handle them. I'm not a boy," Itzkowitz answered firmly. "But it's good that you told me all this. Thank you! I'll repay you." And glancing at Elya, he said as if astonished, "I see that you're a true Maskil, a really true one!"

"Right, a true one," Elya agreed.

"How did you become a Maskil?"

"Ah! There is much to tell; writing about it would fill a whole book," Elya said excitedly. "One-and-a-half years ago I was still a religious fanatic. I'd definitely have remained blind my whole life had God not made a miracle for me. Five months ago, my uncle who lives in G. married off his daughter. My father traveled to the wedding and took me along, and at the wedding I got to know the groom's brother. What a man he is! What a man! There's no one in the world like him. Maybe you've heard of him? His name is Artzik Goldman."

"No. I don't know him."

"Well, to make a long story short, he took to me, as they say, with both hands! In the beginning, of course, I didn't want to hear anything. I argued with him. But he sat down next to me, held me in a vise, and forced thoughts into my head. He explained to me what the Haskalah is. Then he gave me a book to read. . . . You know which? *Hato'eh Be-darkhe Ha-hayim* by Peretz Smolenskin. A Wanderer on the Path of Life. Have you heard of it? It's the only book of its kind in the entire world! It opened my eyes. I became a completely different person. If you'd have read this book!"

"I have read it." Itzkowitz smiled.

"You read it? I can't believe it! Well? What do you say? It's . . . It's a real gem. Afterwards, Goldman gave me another book, a historical novel. *The Love of Zion*. You probably read that, too."

"Certainly. By Abraham Mapu."

"I brought that book with me here; I've already read it three times. I remember nearly all of it by heart. It's true, there isn't as much depth in this book as there is in *A Wanderer on the Path of Life*. But the language, the style, it's practically honey! My heart swelled as I read it."

"Did he maybe also tell you about Smolenskin's *Burial of the Ass* and Lilienblum's *Sins of the Youth*?" Itzkowitz asked with a smile.

"Yeah. He mentioned them," Elya cried. "Did you read those books, too? And here I thought they're impossible to get hold of."

"Nah, it's not a big deal. You can get them . . . And quite easily, too," Itzkowitz said in the same even tone, and bending over, he pulled out from beneath the divan a bound package of Hebrew books.

"You have them!" Elya burst out, astonished. "Oh! What joy! Will you lend them to me?"

"Listen," Itzkowitz said solemnly, "You know quite well, don't you, what it means to have such books in your possession? You're asking me to give them to you, but what if they find them on you?"

"Oh, you don't have to worry about that. I know how to hide . . ."

"But still, if they *do* find them? How can I know that you won't reveal who gave them to you?"

"Me?" Elya asked, shocked. "You think I'd say who gave them to me? Am I out of my mind? I'd rather let them tear me to pieces than betray you!"

"Promise me by all that's holy to you that you'll show these books to no one. No one!"

"No, wait," Elya stopped him. "I have a younger brother who's becoming a maskil, too. I'm opening his eyes. Let me give the books only to him. He can keep a secret."

"OK, fine. But no one else. Swear!"

Elya stuck out his hand. "I swear by all that's holy. I swear by the holy Haskalah that I won't show the books to anyone and even if they tear me limb from limb, I won't tell who I got them from."

Elya's vow calmed Itzkowitz, and painstakingly, with a certain solemnity, he untied the package and handed *Sins of the Youth* to Elya. "Take it. Guard it as if it were the apple of your eye."

13

Elya gripped the book. His expression avid, he burrowed into it and began to leaf through its pages. Suddenly, with an air of religious ecstasy, he pressed the book to his lips.

"When you finish reading it and return it, I'll give you another one," Itzkowitz said.

Elya unbuttoned his shirt collar, placed the book against his chest, buttoned up his shirt again, and cried out passionately, "I can't wait till evening, when everyone will be asleep. I'll lock myself up in a room and read all night long."

Then, calming down somewhat, he sat down and began to speak more practically. "I haven't discussed the main thing with you. I told you I've already freed myself from religion, but that's not enough. What do I do next?"

"You must study. Ask your father to let you come and study with me. I won't charge much," Itzkowitz advised him.

"What are you talking about?" Elya cried. "You don't know my father! His goal is to turn me into a rabbi; he keeps me at the Gemara night and day, and he's getting ready to marry me off . . . You can't imagine how much I've already suffered in the last few months. It's like I'm in a grave. Day and night I sit with a Gemara while my soul is swallowed up by the Haskalah. I can't anymore! I've decided to run away from home. What do you think?"

"It's easy to run away, but where will you go?"

"I don't know. To a big city somewhere, where there are other Maskilim."

"How will you live?"

"I'm not worried about that," Elya answered calmly. "I'll manage. How much do I need anyway? Besides, if I fall in with others like us, they'll support me."

"Heaven forbid! Don't rely on that," Itzkowitz cried. "I've already had some experience with this. Yeah, Maskilim, Maskilim! Sure, they're enlightened, but when it comes to their pockets, they stop being Maskilim. You have to wrest every kopeck out of them with pliers."

"Why?" Elya asked in innocent wonder.

"Because the ruble is precious to everyone. To freethinkers and fanatics alike."

"Well, it's not a big deal, anyway. For the first stretch, I have enough. I've been saving money for a long time and I've stashed away eight rubles. After that, I'll see. I won't be destitute," he said firmly. "Look, I have no other choice. It's impossible to stay here any longer. I must find my way into the main den of the Haskalah. Oh, Haskalah, Haskalah, you daughter of heaven!" he cried out poetically. "I envision it like a distant wide sea where gigantic boats are floating."

"Shush. Don't shout. Everyone can hear you. People are surely up already."

"Right. I'd completely forgotten where I am. If only you knew how happy I am I've met you. Now I'm not afraid anymore. I know you'll teach me, show me the way . . . The worst part is that it's very hard to sneak in here unnoticed. In the middle of the week, I can't ever really get away."

He glanced at the window and said, "It's getting dark. I hadn't realized how much time has passed. I have to run. I'm sure my father has left for the synagogue already. Well, take care."

After Elya very cautiously took his leave, Itzkowitz paced excitedly around his room for a long time. He remembered the fantasies of his friends in Vitebsk and his own promises to get some "work" done in Miloslavka. Cheerfully, he said to himself, "Good! We'll see. I'll bring so much enlightenment into town that they'll have plenty to sing about!"

14

On Sunday Itzkowitz began his work. Taking with him several readers, some handwriting samples he'd prepared earlier, and a ruler and pencil, he left for his early morning lessons.

His first lesson was at Zalmen Isser's. In the end, Zalmen Isser had decided to send to Itzkowitz the older one, who already knew how to read well but didn't know grammar, as well as his two younger daughters. When the tutor arrived, he found his three students already at the table, where all the writing instruments, a Russian alphabet book, and a *Sovremennik* journal were laid out. The younger children, washed and combed, were sitting respectfully at the table, awaiting the teacher.

The tutor began his lesson: he drew lines on a sheet of paper, wrote several letters on the first line, and told the children to copy the letters, showing them how to hold the pen. Then he turned to the oldest, Ettel. "Can you tell me what we are starting with?"

"I think . . . with grammar, right away," Ettel began hesitantly, "but I don't have a grammar text. I couldn't get one anywhere. Father is friendly with the district police officer, and he'll go to him today and ask him. He'll definitely have a grammar text."

"Until you get a grammar text, we'll work on dictation. It's also very important."

He began to dictate to her from his book of Krylov's fables, comparing each of the words she'd written with the book to see if she was writing them correctly. While he dictated the entire fable to her, he corrected her mistakes and then assigned her to rewrite the fable three times and study it by heart. This is the way he himself had been taught.

"Please tell me the definitions of the words that I don't understand," Ettel implored him. "Here. I wrote down the words that I don't understand." And she showed him a page on which were written the Russian words for *discomfited*, *birchen*, *grove*, and *enthusiasm*.

"These are perfectly simple words," Itzkowitz interrupted her, somewhat impatiently. "It's quite easy to define them. But what's the point? On this page, you'll find these words; on the next page, you'll find others—"

"So what?"

"So you shouldn't be reading difficult books. You should be reading Paulson's book and then maybe an elementary reader—that sort of book. Only afterwards, when you understand these books well should you start reading thick books and even novels."

"But I do understand what I'm reading. I understand the subject matter very well," Ettel tried protesting. "I can tell you what I just read—"

"Are you arguing with me? Who knows better, me or you?" The tutor grew angry at her and began to teach the younger children to read syllable by syllable. (Their sister had already taught them the alphabet.)

When the lesson was over, Ettel rather diffidently asked the tutor, "At least explain to me the meaning of only these two words: *grove* and *arbor*. Only these two words."

"*Grove*. That's simple: it's a woods. And an *arbor* is a sort of place where ships stop," Itzkowitz answered firmly.

"Thank you very much," Ettel said, pleased.

The second lesson was at Menachem and Tzirel's place. Notwithstanding how late it was, he found the children still at breakfast.

"Would you like some tea?" Tzirel asked him.

"Thank you," he said, accepting the offer.

Tzirel poured him a glass of tea, and, nodding toward the younger girl, she said with maternal pride, "She's a genius, may no evil eye harm her. Yesterday, this old man was at our house, and she made all kinds of faces at him, so he said to her, 'Listen, don't act silly. I'm a matchmaker and if you make faces at me, I'll tell all the potential grooms and nobody will want to marry you.' So she answered him . . . Rivka'le, what did you answer?"

"I answered him, 'If Father will give me a dowry of lots of money, a boy will want me even with my ugly faces.'"

Tzirel and the children smiled broadly at Rivka'le's brilliance. Itzkowitz, too, smiled for courtesy's sake.

When they finished drinking tea, the tutor seated the children and began to show them how to write. Tzirel joined them at the table, and each time the tutor made a comment, she piped up, "Zelda'le, do you hear what he's saying to you?" Or: "Gnendele, use your head. I'm paying money for this. . . ."

The third lesson was at the Rosenavs', where Chana Leah's granddaughter and a neighbor's daughter were also supposed to join. When the tutor walked in, all the children were already there, sitting on the floor and playing with little stones. When they noticed him, they jumped up and began to dance for joy: "The tutor's here! The tutor's here!"

15

The fourth lesson was at Gnessa Yachnes's house, where her children were joined by the daughter of Leib and Shifra, whose ability to pay Chana Leah had questioned. At this lesson, no writing materials had been prepared. The children ran to their mothers, but they soon returned teary-eyed and without paper and pen.

Behind them strode the mothers.

"They came running like madmen," Gnessa Yachnes complained, "asking us to give them paper, pens, ink, and I don't know what else!"

"But they have to have all those things," the tutor said.

"You hear that? Money again! I didn't think I needed to provide all this stuff; I figured you'd bring all of it with you."

"That's not what we discussed. This is how it's done everywhere: the mothers buy the paper and notebooks themselves. You can ask anyone."

"I told you this before, didn't I," Shifra said to Gnessa. "If you start with these tutors, you'll never be able to get rid of them."

"Well, then, how much do they need? Just tell me," Gnessa said, furious, and gave the children a few kopecks.

All these lessons took till two in the afternoon and exhausted Itzkowitz terribly. Each hour seemed like an eternity, and after the fourth lesson, he barely dragged himself home; he was pale, had a headache, and was so exhausted he barely ate anything for lunch.

He still had three appointments scheduled for the afternoon: with the blonde Esther Dvoshe, then early evening at Yosel's cheder, and finally, at the end of the day, with Melech Akiva, to write his love letters.

When the tutor arrived at Esther Dvoshe's house, she dashed about the room as if she'd been shot, berating the maid who'd been puttering in the parlor, jostling her out of the room and into the kitchen. Then, Esther Dvoshe extended her hand to the tutor. Panting, she said fervidly, "I have been waiting for you."

She seated the tutor next to her and informed him that she wanted to learn everything all at once, but they would have to start with a thorough German lesson. Itzkowitz, already familiar with her weakness for German, had come prepared with a cleanly written German alphabet. The girl was captivated by it. With a strained expression on her face, she began to copy out the letters, and after she completed each letter she pointed to it and asked the tutor, "Is that good?" But soon she grew tired of this activity and demanded that the tutor show her how to do a mathematical calculation. Itzkowitz began to explain to her how to write numbers. Understanding none of it, she kept mimicking everything he said, and when he asked, "Do you understand?" she quickly responded, "Of course. What's not to understand?"

Then she demanded a sample of Russian handwriting. As she sat bent over the sheet of paper, copying out the letters, Esther Dvoshe suddenly touched Itzkowitz's leg with her own. Itzkowitz turned red, but he didn't move his leg. Breathing heavily, the girl pointed at what she'd written and asked, her voice quivering with excitement, "Is . . . is it good?"

"Very good," Itzkowitz replied in the same excitable tone, and he, too, as if by mistake, pressed his leg against hers.

In the other room, the clock hoarsely struck five o'clock. But Itzkowitz didn't want to leave yet, so he continued to sit there for another quarter of an hour. When at last he rose to go, Esther Dvoshe said unhappily, "You're leaving already? It's not even an hour."

"Heaven forbid! I wouldn't leave before it's time. But I heard the clock strike five."

Esther Dvoshe went into the other room, quickly moved the clock hand to a quarter to five, then returned and said to the tutor, "Please, come in here, and you'll see it's only four forty-five. We still have a quarter of an hour."

Itzkowitz stayed for another quarter of an hour and then left, his mind in a strange, feverish turmoil.

At Yosel's cheder, he had three students. As for the fourth boy in the cheder, his parents not only didn't let him study, but they even refused to allow him to remain in the classroom during Itzkowitz's lesson.

In the cheder, Itzkowitz suddenly relaxed. With boys he felt comfortable and at home, not like with girls.

Yosel greeted the tutor with a sour little smile. Deep inside him, he'd been carrying around enlightened thoughts for a while now. He'd hoped to benefit from the tutor's knowledge, and had even thought about possibly getting a taboo book from him sometime. Yosel had been longing to read one of these forbidden enlightened books—in secret, of course. But all those sinful thoughts had lurked within him only until that discussion in the synagogue. The accusation by the scribe's son that he was siding with the tutor had so scared Yosel that he forgot all his enlightened thoughts and resolved to help get the tutor back onto the path of righteousness. So, as the tutor came in now, a struggle commenced in the melamed's soul between his secret desires and the sober voice of prudence.

Let Isser start working on the tutor first, he thought to himself. *In the meantime, I'll stand quietly off to the side.*

He explained to the tutor at some length how he'd been teaching the children Russian up till now. He himself was bad at reading, but he'd nevertheless taught the children to read by sounding out syllables. As far as handwriting was concerned, he hadn't been able to teach capital letters because he himself couldn't write them, but the children were able to write lowercase letters quite decently. He then showed the tutor the children's notebooks.

Itzkowitz scanned the notebooks with a sort of gracious pride and politely showed Yosel that the letters **Й** and **Ч** were missing from his alphabet.

"I didn't know how to pronounce them," Yosel answered innocently.

Then Itzkowitz showed him that the **Ц** could be written in two ways—with a header above it or with an edge at the bottom—and that the letter **Ч** was supposed to be after **ф**.

"Nevertheless," he concluded, "it's written quite well, and the handwriting isn't bad, either."

After the lesson, before Itzkowitz had even managed to stand up, Yosel, who'd been sitting in a corner the entire time, snapped: "Quick, children, clean everything off the table and take out the Gemaras."

In the courtyard, Melech, the fiancé, was already waiting for Itzkowitz. When he spotted Itzkowitz, he murmured, "Follow me, but quietly," and led the tutor up to his attic room. There, he carefully shut the door and handed Itzkowitz two letters written in Russian in a large, though quite soft, feminine handwriting.

"Please. Read it and translate every word for me."

Itzkowitz began to read Melech's fiancée's letter. It was almost illiterate, but very pretentious. The bride wrote him that she was reading "very interesting novels of which she was greatly enamored." Clumsily, with much meandering, she tried to narrate the plot of one of the romance novels. She then expressed the desire for her fiancé to court her, to "begin a romance" with her, despite the fact that they'd already signed a contract and were engaged to be married. Both letters were signed, "From me, your dear bride, Sonya Khalef." All the way on the bottom, there was a postscript in Yiddish. In the first letter: "Please remember, for God's sake, to respond in Russian. I assume the matchmaker wasn't lying when she told me you knew Russian and even German." And in the second letter:

"My father has asked me again to remind your father about the seventy-five rubles he was supposed to put in the bank for the dowry."

Reading, translating, and explaining the letter took more than an hour, but Melech wasn't satisfied with Itzkowitz's explanations and kept looking for clues and hidden meanings in every word and phrase. "What's the meaning of this?" he kept asking. "What's behind that?"

Once Itzkowitz had finished reading the letters, Melech said solemnly, "Well then, take the pen and write whatever I tell you on this piece of paper." He dictated the following letter to Itzkowitz:

> Pretty flower growing in the beautiful vineyard of the city of Minsk, Sonya Khalef, may your light shine!
>
> Like a wide stream, which flows between tall shores and cannot flood the valley—that is how I aspire to look at your face but cannot, because I am in Miloslavka, and you—in Minsk. Oh! Bitter lot! When will I live to see this happy time? And just like the sun shines only during the day, but at night we don't get to see it for all the money in the world, that is how I, too, don't get to see your sumptuous figure. Oh! Bitter lot!

"You said these words already," Itzkowitz commented.

"True. But it doesn't matter; write them again. Words like these can even be written twice . . . Well, how do you like my elegant style?"

"Good! Excellent!" Itzkowitz praised sincerely.

"For two nights I've been thinking about these words . . . mulling them over . . . So, what do I write next?"

"I think you have to write to her about the books you're reading and about this thing she's requesting . . . that you should, with her . . . how should I say it, well, start this romance with her," Itzkowitz, in a bit of a spot, replied.

"What does it mean, to start a romance? Honestly, I don't understand what the meaning of it is."

"Quite simple: write her love letters, you know, love. You write that you're in love, that you miss her, and you call her pretty names."

Melech scratched his head and was quiet for a while. Then he said, "What do you mean? I'm already writing her love letters. Isn't this enough? Okay, take the pen and write this: 'My much beloved bride! As to your request that I start a romance with you, I will fulfill it with the greatest of pleasure, although in four months from now, our wedding will take place, God willing, and none of this will any longer be necessary.'"

16

Several days later, when Itzkowitz came home for lunch, he found Chana Leah extremely perturbed. She furtively called him into another room and in a voice tinged with terror, she whispered, "They were here to call you to the. . . . police district."

"Me?" Itzkowitz asked, turning pale.

"Yes. I'm afraid it's because of a passport."

"I have a passport."

"You do?" the woman cried out happily. "Oh, thank God! I was so worried. How would I know you have a passport?"

"Oh, and what a passport I have!" Itzkowitz said, as if he himself couldn't believe it. "When did the district officer want me to come?"

"The goy said very soon."

Despite his owning a passport, Itzkowitz didn't feel at all reassured about the impending visit. "Oh, please don't let him pick on me for no reason," he said, frightened. "Devil knows he can pick a quarrel over the smallest trifle."

"No, our district officer is a good goy. He just wants a few rubles. What can we do? But there's one thing that puzzles me: how did he find out about you?"

"Looks like some good people thought it important to inform him . . . You said a few rubles? How much?"

"Whatever works. Take along three, but try to give him only one. If he refuses, then too bad, you'll have to give him more. That's how it's done."

Itzkowitz was so distraught he couldn't eat any lunch, and taking a three-ruble coin from Chana Leah, he left to the police superintendent.

The administrative office of the superintendent was on the other side of town, where only Christians lived. The superintendent's office and home occupied a spacious building.

Even the outside of the administrative office, the mere sight of the Russian coat of arms and the eagle, terrified Itzkowitz. He took his passport out of his wallet, and gripping it as if it were some sort of safety belt, he opened the door and hastily removed his hat.

He found himself in a large waiting room. Five or six provincial men—police officers—were either sitting or half lying on the benches.

"Who're you looking for?" one of the officers asked him, eyeing him with curiosity.

"The superintendent. . . . His Honor . . . said to come," Itzkowitz stammered.

"Is he a Jew, or is he not a Jew?" one officer whispered to another, snickering.

A massive figure appeared in the doorway leading to the administrative office. He wasn't wearing a suit jacket. He had a fleshy face with huge facial features and a double chin, somewhat grey whiskers, and bulging eyes. At first glance, his appearance made a chilling impression.

"Who's here?" he asked in a hoarse bass voice, scanning the room.

The huge figure and formidable voice made Itzkowitz tremendously agitated. He straightened up and barely managed to stammer out the words in Russian, "Your . . . Honor . . . summoned," and then held out his passport.

The superintendent gaped at Itzkowitz, astonished. Suddenly, he said, "Oh, are you the tutor?"

"Yes, that's me."

The superintendent burst out laughing. Then he said cheerfully, "Well, well. Welcome, Mr. Tutor, I am very pleased to see you!"

Itzkowitz entered the administrative office. A young gentile was sitting at a table and kept writing without even looking up.

"Sit," the superintendent said, indicating a chair next to a table piled high with papers. "What's that?" he asked, as he noticed the folded paper in Itzkowitz's extended hand. "A passport? Good. Let's see." Opening it, he began to read, as if it were a mere formality: "Zalmen Leibov Itzkowitz . . . Itzkowitz, well, fine, but let's leave this for later." And he returned the passport to Itzkowitz. "So you've come, shall we say, to Miloslavka to work as a tutor? A fine occupation. But are you a tutor or a melamed?"

"No, no, not a melamed. A tutor."

"You teach Russian grammar? Do you have a permit?" he asked unexpectedly. But noticing the fear on Itzkowitz's face, he quickly added, "Oh, don't be scared!

I'll ignore it. I'll let that slip. Teach, teach! As much as you want. By God, with all my heart I'm happy you've come here to this town. Not that you can make our little Jews become grammarians! They're such primitive people, don't you think?"

"Very primitive. They know nothing about education," Itzkowitz replied with more boldness, now that the superintendent's words had calmed him and given him courage.

"True, true. All they know about is the synagogue and again the synagogue . . . Each a greater swindler than the next. Word of honor! . . . You smoke?"

"Yes." Now Itzkowitz became entirely confident, and taking the cigarette the superintendent handed him, he quickly and clumsily smoked it.

"And on the Sabbath? Do you smoke then, too?" the superintendent asked with a sarcastic smile. "Uh oh, it's forbidden!"

"I smoke when nobody's looking," Itzkowitz replied, smiling.

"Really? Upon my word! Ha-ha! What if the rabbi finds out? He'll raise quite a ruckus. 'Oh, woe is me,' he'll cry. 'Why are you smoking a cigarette on the Sabbath?' Eh?"

"Ha-ha."

"But it doesn't make any difference," the superintendent said cheerfully, pumping Itzkowitz on his shoulder. "Don't be scared of them. If any of them bother you, come to me right away, and I'll very quickly teach them proper behavior. They're terrified of me. I know them well. Long sidelocks and beasts through and through. Isn't that true?"

With a flatterer's smile, Itzkowitz looked at the superintendent and unsure how to answer, he stammered out in Russian, "*Fanatikeri! Takia fanatikeri tshtshu strost!* Fanatics! Such fanatics. Terrible!"

"You're supposed to say *fanatiki*, not *fanatikeri*," the superintendent corrected him. "So! I'm always getting into scuffles with them. I have a good friend in town; his name is Zalmen Isser. You know him, you teach his children. He came here to borrow a grammar text from me. It just so happened that I had an old grammar book, so I gave it to him. Anyway. I'm always arguing with this Zalmen Isser. Why, I say, don't you eat pork? What kind of sin could it be? A sin is what comes out of your mouth, not what goes in. But he tosses his sidelocks and shouts, 'Ay, woe is me. *Kak moznu*, how can one bear this?' Ha-ha!"

The superintendent stood up, went over to the door, and yelled, "Agasha! Bring in the carafe, a few glasses, and something to eat." Then turning back to the table, he said, "You won't say no to a drink, surely?"

"I won't say no to a drink," Itzkowitz replied, thinking it best to respond only with the same words that were said to him, in order not to make errors in his Russian. Incidentally, it seemed to him that the superintendent spoke in a not quite correct Russian: this sort of Russian language with this sort of accent was one he'd never yet heard. He was in particular convinced that in regards to the word *fanatikeri*, the superintendent was actually mistaken. Naturally, he had no intention of arguing his point, but he clearly knew you didn't say *fanatiki* but *fanatikeri*. He'd already heard the word numerous times. *Fanatikeri*—that meant a religious Jew. And how would the superintendent know a Jewish word like that?

"Yes, young man," the superintendent continued, "I'm very happy that you're settling down here. At least there'll be one educated person to exchange a word with, to confide in. . . . You can't imagine what a backwater this is: there's no social life, no one to play a game of cards with, even. It's enough to make you howl like a wolf, such vexation! The one and only person possible to hang out with, talk, drink a bit—is the priest, the Holy Father. There's another teacher here, but she's very uninteresting, so ugly it's frightful!"

A barefoot gentile woman brought in whiskey and some snacks.

The superintendent smiled and rubbed his hands together contentedly. Then he poured two glasses, took one for himself and gave the other to Itzkowitz.

"To your health! As you say, *l'chaim!*"

"*L'chaim, l'chaim,*" Itzkowitz replied happily. He stood up, took a sip and, as if he'd been burnt, he burst out, "Oy!" and placed the glass with the schnapps on the table.

"What? Did it burn you?" the superintendent asked.

"Like fire!"

"That's why it's *pertzovka!*[1] It's spiced with pepper! Well, eat something. But because I'm an ethical person, I'm telling you in advance that this is pork. Po-or-rk. Ha-ha! Have you ever eaten pork? Admit it!"

---

1. A pepper vodka.

Itzkowitz winked slyly and whispered, "I've already eaten plenty. When no one was looking." And he took a piece of pork.

Never before in his life had Itzkowitz sat in conversation with a Russian non-Jew, especially a regional police superintendent, a man he'd always envisioned in his fantasies as a dreadful hurricane that hurls and shrieks, as an omnipotent force that arrests, strikes, locks you up in prison; and here was that very powerful giant, sitting with him and having a discussion with him as if he were his equal. He didn't know how to behave, what to do with himself. At each word the superintendent uttered, Itzkowitz pulled himself up, straining to demonstrate great attentiveness. The liquor caused a drumming in his head, and he was suddenly struck by the desire to tell the superintendent his biography: how he'd become a Maskil, how he'd been compelled to pretend, and how he later suffered for it. He wanted the superintendent to understand that he'd legitimately earned the attention the superintendent was showing him.

"I came here from Vitebsk," he began. "In Vitebsk there are different sorts of people, very different. Everyone is very accomplished. They don't pray, they smoke on the Sabbath—everything! They study, they read heretical and Russian books, and all kinds of other books. Over there . . . I can't describe it! It's a whole other world. An open world. Education . . . Only education!"

The superintendent listened to his choppy phrases and thought his own thoughts.

"So, you're saying it's a whole other kind of life in Vitebsk," he said, sighing. "Of course! A city with a regular provincial government. And they've gone and stuck me here in this hole. And they've kept me here—this is the seventh year already!—until I'm already overgrown with moss."

He stood up and gave Itzkowitz his hand. "Well, I'm very happy to have gotten to know you. Teach. Teach your little Jews, it's very good! And if anyone insults you, come to me immediately. Don't even say a word to them. I'll stick up for you."

As he escorted the tutor out of the building, he added, "Come visit me more often. In the evenings, or in your free time. You'll be a welcome guest. I'll introduce you to the priest. A highly educated person!"

Itzkowitz left the superintendent in a sublime mood. What a welcome! Plus, the superintendent had even promised to stick up for him against any injustices that came his way. And, on top of all that, the three-ruble coin had remained in his wallet!

"Well, now I'm laughing at all of them," Itzkowitz said to himself, thinking about the Hebrew teachers. "Now they won't dare touch me."

He decided he would continue to pay visits to the superintendent.

17

To Itzkowitz, the first week of giving lessons felt like an eternity. Despite his extremely elementary "pedagogical method," he still couldn't make the lessons run smoothly. His entire pedagogy consisted of these simple steps: he showed the letters of the alphabet to the students or read with each student for a few minutes; then he drew lines on a sheet of paper, wrote a letter or a few words on the first line, and told his students to copy them. The teaching of arithmetic, too, was limited, at this point, to the mere writing of numbers. In spite of this, there was constant chaos and racket during the lessons. The children all spoke at once, making the tutor's head spin. One of them showed him every single letter separately to ask whether it was written well; another asked him to line a sheet of paper; a third complained that her friend had punched her; a fourth absolutely needed him to tell her who was writing better, she or her friend. And so on.

Itzkowitz couldn't cope. Not only were the students difficult, but so were their parents and relatives, who—right from the start—were suspicious of him and scrutinized every detail of his job. The mothers haggled with him over every kopeck ad nauseam: *Why was the paper necessary? The ink? Never mind the books.* In their eyes, the expenses were pure thievery on the tutor's part. Itzkowitz, on the other hand, simply didn't have the necessary chutzpah to wheedle these things out of them. In the room where the lessons took place, people who didn't belong kept coming in, sticking their noses into the lessons and fooling around with the children, and the tutor didn't have the courage to kick out the uninvited guests. Often, a sister or brother of the student would come in during the lesson and clamor: "Chana'ke, Mother said you should run to the store for kasha right now! You'll finish writing later."

"Oh, no, my dear, I just want to write one more line," the girl would beg.

"You rascal! You'll soon get a few smacks! Get going. This very minute! Teacher, tell her to go."

"If you're told to go, go," the tutor would say, forced to consent.

Or the mistress of the house would run in and yell angrily, "Clean up your writing stuff, and make it snappy. I need this room. You'll finish writing tomorrow."

And the lesson would be cut short.

The most difficult appointments for Itzkowitz were the ones at Zalmen Isser's and at Melech the fiancé. Once Ettel acquired a grammar text, she began to study diligently and kept posing questions that perplexed the tutor, causing him embarrassment. He also got aggravated by her requests for definitions of the words they were reading. In order to maintain his prestige, he answered her in a confident tone, improvising or defining the words he was unfamiliar with according to what he thought they must mean or according to their similarity to another word. He answered her with such authority that it never dawned on the girl to doubt his mastery of the topic at hand. But the odd explanations and definitions disoriented her, made the contents of what she was reading ambiguous, and brought her to the conclusion that she was incapable of understanding anything. Her thirst for knowledge, her diligence, and serious approach toward her lessons so irritated Itzkowitz, that he grew to despise her. He couldn't bear her earnestly questioning expression and would meanly interrupt her while she was talking.

At Melech's, on the other hand, he had other annoyances. Melech was so pleased with his first letter to his bride that without waiting for a response from her, he decided to write another letter the next day because he'd thought of another pretty flowery phrase. So Itzkowitz had to devote the next evening to him, too. Every day for the rest of the week, the same thing happened. Finally, Itzkowitz grew infuriated and explained to him that he couldn't devote three hours every day to him. Melech tried to argue that their agreement had specified "an average" amount of time, but Itzkowitz, aware that he needed him, held firmly to his decision, and he succeeded in setting limits on Melech's literary ardor.

At Esther Dvoshe's, the lesson would be conducted under strange circumstances. Between the teacher and the student there had developed the sort of relationship that made the hour fly by unnoticed. The lesson served merely as an opportunity for a particular kind of flirtation between them: quite "unexpectedly" their legs would press against one another under the table, their hands would touch, their shoulders, their faces would angle toward one another. Throughout the lesson, the teacher and the student were always in a cloud, not hearing what the other was saying, turning red one minute, pale the next, and each of them secretly thinking about exchanging a kiss. But they couldn't make up their minds to do it.

Itzkowitz's most enjoyable lesson was the one at Yosel's cheder. Here he felt at home. He'd joke with the students using Gemara interpretations, and he'd regale Yosel with various facts about his own teaching, which had much in common with the job of a melamed, a cheder teacher. Once, after the lesson, Itzkowitz asked Yosel, "Which tractate are you teaching now?"

"*Chulin.*"

"Ah, on slaughtering animals." Itzkowitz knew the tractate well and eagerly asked which page they were up to. When Yosel told him, Itzkowitz—after some reflection—recalled the text on that page and told Yosel what it was about without ever consulting the page. The students and Yosel were astonished.

"W-wow," Yosel burst out. "I see it's true; you're quite a scholar."

"What, do you think a tutor must generally be an ignoramus?"

"Heaven forbid, but . . . Anyway, since it is what it is, I want to ask you a few questions about this very tractate."

"Certainly! Certainly! I want to ask you a few questions, too. But unfortunately, I have no time today."

The next day Itzkowitz remained during the Hebrew lesson, posed questions to the children, and then provided answers for them. The children were enamored of him. Afterwards, he and Yosel debated the fine points of Talmudic law, and both of them demonstrated expertise and brilliance. Neither bested the other, but they each debated plenty.

For a while Yosel sat quietly, smiling and stroking his beard. Then, calmly, with a bit of regret in his tone, he said, "It's not right! Tell yourself whatever you want, but you're not in the right place. For crying out loud! You could've been an amazing melamed. Wait, what am I saying? Even a rabbi! And you chose tutoring! What a waste."

Flattered by the praise, Itzkowitz replied with a little smile, "So what?! I know it myself: I had the potential to become a rabbi. But what could I do if this was my destiny?"

"What do you mean, destiny? For issues like these, there's no such thing as destiny," Yosel replied.

"Oh, there's a lot to tell and too little time to hear it," Itzkowitz said. "During the semester recess, I'll tell you in detail how I ended up tutoring. Then you'll understand."

The next day—it was a Friday—Yosel met Isser in the synagogue and told him about his discussion with the tutor.

"I'm sure it'll be really easy to 'drag' what we want out of him," Isser remarked. "All we have to do is apply ourselves properly. I'll invite him for tea along with a few other people, as well. You come, too, and we'll get started on him."

Next Shabbos in the synagogue, Itzkowitz was feeling much more at ease. He looked everyone straight in the eye and nobody gave him angry, accusing glances as on the previous Shabbos.

During the reading of the Torah, Isser came over to him. "How come we haven't seen you all week?" he said in mild reproach. "Are you already that busy that you don't even have time to come to prayers? Just remember: how many opportunities to say 'Amen' have you squandered! Isn't that a loss for you? It adds up to a huge fortune!" And he burst out laughing.

"No, honestly," he continued, "I've been wanting to meet you. I want to invite you over for a cup of tea. Come visit me. Don't put it off too long."

"Thank you," Itzkowitz answered, and thought: *Yeah, I get what you want to do. You're spreading out a net to trap me. But I'm too shrewd for that!*

18

Several days later, after Itzkowitz had finished that day's lesson, Yosel approached him with a suggestion: "If you feel like it, you can teach the children the Hebrew lesson today instead of me. I'd really like to hear how you explain it to them."

"Sure," Itzkowitz gladly agreed, and taking Yosel's place, he—to the children's great pleasure—began to explain the topic discussed in the Gemara, a topic instantly familiar to him. Yosel stood off to the side and listened with a smile. Right away, Itzkowitz got into the role, took on the tone of a melamed, and for an entire hour, he studied with the children, explaining to them a section of the Gemara, along with its commentaries.

The truth was, Yosel was disappointed by what he could see of Itzkowitz's scholarship; he'd been expecting more. In spite of this, he made an effort to express his enthusiasm and shower Itzkowitz with praise.

Once Yosel sent the children home, he asked Itzkowitz to stay, and they returned to their earlier discussion. "No, I'm telling you again, I can't understand how a person like you was able to abandon the Torah.

Say whatever you want, but there's no way I can understand it."

"I already told you, there's a lot to tell and little time to hear it," Itzkowitz replied.

"I believe you that there's a lot to tell. But that there's little time to hear it, forgive me, *that* I don't believe. Go ahead! Honestly, I really want to hear about it. We haven't known each other a long time, but you're as dear to me as an old friend, you're like family. . . ."

Moved by Yosel's words, Itzkowitz wanted to tell him his life story. But since he couldn't divulge the entire truth, he decided to relate his "history" with a few improvements.

"The person at fault for all of this is the dean of my yeshiva. A real thief! It's completely his fault. He slaughtered me!" Itzkowitz spoke with fervor, truly believing that the dean was responsible for all his problems.

"The dean, eh," Yosel wondered aloud, and inched closer to Itzkowitz.

"I admit I was a yeshiva boy. For five years I studied in a yeshiva. I don't mean to brag, but I was the best student; people raved about me. Anyway, you understand how it is nowadays. So I wanted to learn a bit of Russian, too. So what? Is that a sin?"

"No," Yosel answered firmly. "You see I also know a bit of Russian. My only regret is that I never learned more."

"So, you see! Anyway, I began to learn a little something for an hour or so a day between the afternoon and evening prayers. And the beadle noticed and tattled to the dean. To make a long story short, the dean called me into his office and began to yell at me and berate me, and he called me a heretic. Well, I'm hot-tempered, too. And I don't like to be yelled at. So I answered him back. In short, one word followed another, we got into a fight, and I left the yeshiva."

"Aha!" Yosel marveled.

"When the dean calmed down, he sent some people to persuade me to return. But I'm stubborn. With me, if I'm done, it's over. Although actually, I had the best meal plan in town. Still, I gave it up and began to give lessons in Russian."

"Oh, how anger can lead a person astray!" Yosel sighed with bitterness.

"Anyway, I set out on this path. I didn't throw away the Gemara, but I kept entering more and more deeply into the world of secular knowledge. Well, I'm sure you know that these wisdoms are also limitless. . . . Anyway, that's my whole story."

"Wow. What a story. . . ." Yosel said pensively.

"But I'll tell you one thing," Itzkowitz concluded. "No matter how much I studied, no matter how much I got into worldly studies, I've remained a Jew."

"That's the most important thing," Yosel conceded, "to guard the spark inside you. But here's what I want to ask you now: basically, everything resulted from the fact that you lost your temper. But now that your temper has subsided, the question is . . . ," he continued his sentence, intoning the traditional Gemara chant, waiting for Itzkowitz to respond with the logical conclusion.

Itzkowitz burst out laughing. "Ah, I see. You want to bring me back to the proper path, don't you? Come on, be honest!"

"What do you mean, do I want to? Of course I want to! But the way this story goes is, it doesn't depend on my wanting it, but on yours. It's true, I don't really understand why you wouldn't want it?"

Itzkowitz stood up. "Listen to me," he said somberly. "I've thought about it myself. I've thought about it a lot. But there are some reasons I can't divulge . . . In any case, I can tell you that it's completely futile to moralize and reprimand me. I understand everything very well, and when the time comes . . . but what is there to talk about?"

Itzkowitz walked out of the cheder in a good mood. He himself didn't realize that he'd created an entire legend about his past. It felt to him as if he'd genuinely unburdened his heart to Yosel and had been met with empathy and warmth. But simultaneously, he was thrilled that he'd managed to dupe the melamed, that he'd convinced him of his connection to the Torah and so removed any suspicions of his ties to the Haskalah movement.

The next day, when Itzkowitz was sitting in on Yosel's lesson, a boy walked in, holding a little note. Yosel read it and, without saying a word, handed it to Itzkowitz. The letter was from Isser. In it, he asked Yosel to invite "Reb Zalmen"—that is, the tutor—on his behalf, to his home that evening for tea.

"In the evening I'm busy with . . ." Itzkowitz nodded to the side of the courtyard where Melech lived.

"So you'll go to Isser a little later," Yosel suggested. "By then, I'll have sent the children home and I'll join you."

"Somehow, I'm not in the mood."

"Why not? You work all day. Why shouldn't you socialize once in a while? You literally hardly see a live person in front of your eyes. That's not right! Besides, Isser will take it as an insult. After all, he's not just anybody . . . You should go!"

"Well, then, okay, I will," Itzkowitz agreed.

Isser lived in a large two-story house belonging to his father-in-law, Ezriel. He lived in two rooms, but he entertained guests in the large living room. When Yosel and Itzkowitz—having vigorously wiped their shoes on the outside mat—entered the living room, they found a few people already there. Besides Isser, there was Tzipa's husband, Michoel, the old man who'd taken part in the plot against the tutor, and a melamed. Isser and the guests, wearing only their yarmulkes, no hats, sat chatting around a samovar on a large table. When the new guest walked in, Isser rose slightly from his seat and announced: "Welcome! Why are you so late? I was starting to think you weren't coming."

"I was busy," Itzkowitz excused himself.

"How many students do you have that you're so busy all day and night?" Michoel asked. "You must be making a fortune."

"Soon he'll start lending money at interest and will put you out of business," the melamed said to Isser with a flattering little smile.

"Yeah, right, that's exactly what I'm afraid of," Isser answered, and burst into smug laughter.

He invited the guests to sit and handed them some tea. "We were talking about cantors," he told Itzkowitz. "We're about to hire a cantor now, in time for the High Holy days. We pay fifty rubles. How does it work in Vitebsk?"

Itzkowitz stopped drinking and replied quickly, "In Vitebsk, in the Great Synagogue, there's a cantor who sings with a choir. He gets three hundred rubles."

"Three hundred rubles!" they all marveled. "Why do they pay him so much? Does he sing that beautifully?"

"It's not so much for his beautiful singing but because he sings from sheet music."

"Ah! From sheet music. That's a whole other sort of cantor. That's the sort of cantor who sings in the synagogue today and goes where the devil leads him tomorrow . . . like, into theaters. Singing from notes!" Isser mocked. "And if he forgets the notes, he stands there in the middle of the prayer and—doesn't budge! Ha-ha!"

"There's a story about that," Michoel said. "Once, a cantor forgot the most important note in the middle of the prayers. He couldn't remember it, no matter how hard he tried. So he couldn't move ahead, and he couldn't go back. He was stuck—mute. His wife was sitting in the women's section in the balcony, and she remembered the note. But how could she jog her husband's memory? Anyway, she suddenly burst into song in that same tune he couldn't remember. She sang: 'If you do-on't know ho-ow to do it, if you ca-an't do it, do-on't undertake to do-oo it.' So, of course, the cantor heard the tune and was able to continue the prayers."

They all laughed heartily.

"A cantor with notes. Never heard of such a thing," Yosel said. "They say the Berlin cantor is nothing more, nothing less, than a clean-shaven Jew!"

"Not only in Berlin, but even in Vilna, they say there's a cantor like that," Isser said. "In Vilna, obviously, the gang of Maskilim have their own separate synagogue."

"There must be many of them there, right?" the melamed asked.

"Are you kidding? They've got their whole lair there!" Isser cried. "They commit all kinds of terrible deeds. People say that one year on Purim the Maskilim sent the great *Vilna Gaon*, the genius of Vilna, Reb Eliyahu, a small pig for *mishloach manos* instead of the regular basket of food. What do you think the Gaon did? Did he kick the messenger out? No way! He took the small pig, gave the messenger a ruble tip, and even told him to thank them nicely. Naturally, 'they' were dumbfounded. They immediately sent one of their people to the Gaon to find out what this was all about. 'Rabbi,' the man said, 'we don't understand you. We'd assumed you would beat up our messenger and kick him out, but instead, you reward him nicely and even tell him to thank us? How can that be?' The Gaon, brilliant man that he was, replied, 'What do you mean? Why should I kick him out? On the contrary, I was very moved by your gift. You took your favorite food and sent it to me!'"

All of them, including Itzkowitz, burst out laughing.

"Well, and in Vitebsk, are there a lot of Maskilim?" Isser asked suddenly, staring directly into Itzkowitz's eyes.

"How should he know about the Maskilim in Vitebsk?" Yosel asked quickly, unnerved by Isser's blunt question.

"Why shouldn't he know?" Isser asked, now staring right at Yosel. "Idiot, you think that only a Maskil can know about Maskilim?" And turning back to Itzkowitz, he said with a little smile, "I'll tell you the truth. The first time I saw you, I actually thought you were a Maskil, but now I'm beginning to think the opposite: that you're one of the thirty-six hidden righteous men, a *lamed vovnik*."

"What do you think? Is it impossible that I'm one of them?" Itzkowitz asked, laughing.

"What's the point of all this banter? Let's get to the point," Michoel said. "I'll tell you frankly: I'd have been much less surprised if you were a Maskil than— as it seems to me now—that you're actually a regular Jew. Why? A man arrives here wearing a short jacket and without sidelocks. He begins to teach children Russian. Of course, everyone can see what kind of person this is! It's clear: this person has thrown off the burden of Judaism. He has sinned. He's stopped being an upright man. Obviously, we can see who we're dealing with. But if this same tutor with the short jacket and without sidelocks comes into the synagogue, sits down with a Gemara, and claims he's still a religious Jew, then the question naturally comes up: What does this mean? Is it one or the other? You can't have it both ways. Are you a Jew? Then be a regular Jew. If not, admit frankly that you're not. There's a story people tell: Once a Jew, a traveler, walked into an inn early in the morning. He hears the innkeeper woman waking someone: 'Ivan, Ivan, get up. It's time to go to church.'

"The traveler was shocked and asked, 'Jewish woman, why do you care if Ivan is late for church?'

"Now, listen to this! You know what the woman said? The woman says, 'Ivan is my son. He converted to Christianity.'

"The traveler was even more astounded. 'Well, now my question is even greater,' he said. "Why are you, his mother, urging him to go to church?'

"'Eh, eh, sir,' she replied. 'He didn't want to be a real Jew? Fine, so be it. But let him at least be a real goy.' You get it? One or the other. Either this way or that. Because as it stands now—what are you?"

Dejected by the blunt attack, Itzkowitz smiled pitifully, unsure how to respond.

Yosel came to his aid. "No, Reb Michoel, you're wrong. Your analogy doesn't relate to Reb Zalmen. Obviously, we have to know the reasons. You're seeing Reb Zalmen for maybe the second or third time and haven't exchanged two words with him. But I've already had some conversations with him and know his whole story."

"If that's the case," Michoel said, "then it's altogether different. Forgive me. I didn't want to insult you, God forbid."

"Let's leave it alone," Isser interjected. "I've also only spoken to him a little, but I understand him well. It's quite simple. The man lost his way, crawled into God knows where, but still hasn't lost his Jewish spark, and wants to return to the correct path. Now, it all depends on his being helped to return to the Torah and to Judaism. Isn't that true, Zalmen'ke?" he finished, affably slapping Itzkowitz on his shoulder.

"Well, could we say that . . . that . . . it's not as simple as that . . . ," Itzkowitz stammered.

"Listen," Michoel continued, edging closer to the tutor, "let's analyze this situation well: You're a smart young man, you're competent, a scholar; you've studied Gemara for many years. You'd already set out on a certain path, and you could have become a somebody; it would have been simple to reach a higher level . . . And you traded all of this, for what? Forgive me, but for a pot of lentils like Uncle Esau. If, at least, it was a *large* pot of lentils! But no, not even that. Just think about how you're living: all day you run around with your tongue hanging out, you don't have a minute of free time, you work like a horse, struggling and sweating, and you barely manage to eke out a piece of bread. And what about the impression you make? Beautiful, isn't it, that you have to tend to little girls and deal with women who look at you as frivolous. Why're you doing all this? They're saying you want to learn secular wisdom. Well, I ask you, will you get that wisdom from your little girls?"

"You forgot another thing," Isser cut in. He got up, went to the cupboard, took out a flask of liquor and shot glasses, and placed them on the table. "You can't forget, you're not a child anymore, thank God. You have to begin thinking about a wife. Now, if you drag yourself around from house to house and teach girls, what kind of crazy person will want you? But if you'd sit and study Gemara, it wouldn't be hard at all for you to make a good match. Especially with your worldly knowledge! You'd be able to find a bride with a hefty dowry. Afterwards, you'd start making purchases, get into business. It's no small thing, a man with a Gemara brain and writing skills, too! Well, a toast, *l'chaim!*" he concluded, and poured himself a shot. "May God allow us to toast to you throwing away your secular teaching!"

"Amen!" All of them drank to it.

"Listen to me," Isser, chipper after his first glass, said. "Come on, spit on those lessons of yours, chuck your short overcoat, and become a Jew again. Just like that!"

"Listen," Michoel added, "evil is powerful. When it pulls you in, it's hard to escape its clutches. But you have to make an effort! Like Samson, you must yank at the chains till they'll tear into shreds." As he said this, he spread his hands, demonstrating how Samson had ripped the chains.

"Why're you so silent, Reb Zalmen? Everyone's talking and you're not answering," Yosel interjected.

Itzkowitz, sitting there as if confused, shrugged and quickly replied, "I . . . what should I say? Of course . . . but I have to think."

"What's there to think about?" Isser interrupted him.

"No, leave him alone. Let him think."

"You see," Isser continued, "Adam had two sons, Cain and Abel. Cain killed Abel and God cursed Cain. So Adam then began to think: is it worth it to have more children or not? He thought and he thought, all of hundred and twenty years he thought, till he gave birth to Seth. . . . No need to think! It's decided! You're tossing your studies! Let's make another toast!"

"May God allow us to drink at your wedding!" Isser said.

"May God allow us to drink when you rid yourself of this evil spirit and sit down to study Torah," Michoel added.

"Amen! Amen!"

"Hold it! Zalmen hasn't said *Amen*. Another glass!" Isser cried.

They drank for the third time and when Michoel repeated his wish, Itzkowitz answered loudly and with fervor, "Amen, amen!"

19

Drunk and numb, Itzkowitz tottered home. He took long, wobbling strides in zigzag fashion, threw his arms about, and kept repeating loudly, "It doesn't matter. Let it go. Let it go wherever it goes. Itzkowitz is no fool!"

Fragments of the recent conversation rattled around in his head, in his foggy brain; broken phrases caressed his ego and roused his inner self-esteem: *"You're a smart young man, competent . . ." "You could have been a somebody . . ."* These people, these very same people, understood him! In a flash, they were able to assess the kind of person he was! And then, as he remembered Isser's words about a bride, a warm, joyous sensation made his heart tremble. He immediately pictured Esther Dvoshe, with her excited expression and hazy eyes, and he smiled widely and happily.

It was about midnight. The town was asleep. As if reluctantly but absentmindedly, the sickle-shaped moon feebly lit the poor, crooked little streets with their pathetic, squat, little houses sunken in mud. There was something interminably lonesome about what this picture portrayed. It evoked an old forgotten graveyard, its crooked tombstones scattered in disarray.

As he passed the synagogue, Itzkowitz heard someone calling to him in a cautious whisper: "Tutor. Wait."

"Who's that?" Itzkowitz asked, backing away, frightened.

"It's me, Elya. Don't you recognize me?" the boy said, stepping closer.

Itzkowitz recognized him, but couldn't immediately grasp who the boy was and how he came to be here. "What're you doing here?"

"I'm waiting for you. I saw you going in to Isser's and decided to wait till you got back . . . I want to tell you some good news. It'll make you very happy. In the end, I've decided very definitely to run away from home to M.!"

"To M.?" Itzkowitz repeated, not yet understanding clearly what he was talking about. "Why to M.?"

"I heard there are many Maskilim there. Besides, it's far from Miloslavka."

Finally grasping what Elya was talking about, Itzkowitz remembered the discussion they'd had. He was silent for a moment, and then said hesitantly, "Why so suddenly . . . so unexpected?"

"I can't anymore. Every day is like a year. It's like I'm in hell. The Gemara has become repulsive to me, and besides, Father's absolutely set on marrying me off."

"Marrying you off? To some fine bride? With a large dowry?" Itzkowitz asked cheerfully.

"What do I care what kind of bride? Even if she's golden, do I want to get married?"

"If I were in your place, oh, yes, I'd get married! True as I'm a Jew, I'd get married!" Itzkowitz became impassioned. "You can always study later, and in the meantime, you'd have some money."

"You're poking fun," Elya cried, bursting into laughter. "Get married! Sure, that's all I need. Even if I wouldn't have to get married but just stay here another few months, I wouldn't survive, I'd drown myself. Especially now that I've reread *Sins of Youth*! Ah! What a book that is!"

"What a book!" Itzkowitz cut him off, somewhat irritated. "It's a book. Like other books. You become enamored of everything. It'll bring you to no good. Run, you say. It's easy to say, run! It's easier than to think, than to really think something through. That's how all tragedies happen. See here, I ran, too. And got burned. . . . Anyway, do as you see fit. It's late already. Good night."

He walked off hurriedly, leaving Elya astonished and bewildered.

This meeting sobered Itzkowitz up a little. His mood suddenly changed; he began to feel sad and heavy. He walked rapidly, his shoulders stooped, talking to himself with obvious irritation, "Rushing. Always rushing. Crawling into the fire. Haskalah! Enlightenment! Does he understand what the Haskalah is? He'll get caught in a labyrinth like me and won't be able to crawl out of it."

He went upstairs to his room and without undressing, got into bed and soon fell asleep.

The next morning Itzkowitz woke up late with a headache and in a depressed mood. He recalled what had occurred to him the day before, and for just a moment, he thought it had been a dream.

Something very important had occurred, he knew that clearly. But he couldn't collect his thoughts enough to figure out what exactly had happened. *Took me by force, got me drunk, ensnared me in their net* were the phrases floating about in his head. Nevertheless, he felt no complaint, no anger toward them. On the contrary, his tired mind began to justify what had occurred. *Studying, education, the Haskalah*, he thought. Sure, all these things are very beautiful—for those whose bellies are full, who have rich parents. But were they to try—these great Maskilim—to live as I do, to suffer as much as I do, they'd all be singing a different tune.

Once he got dressed and went downstairs, however, and Chana Leah began to talk to him about daily routine tasks, his thoughts soon took another direction. He remembered he had lessons scheduled, had a profession, was financially secure, and yesterday's discussion about returning to the "old" now seemed to him like absurd chatter. What kind of sense did that make? Hale and healthy, and suddenly, go, turn the carriage over, become a yeshiva boy again? You'd have to be crazy! If, at least, he were really the person he'd portrayed himself to Isser and the rest of them, that would be something else. But in reality, he'd already broken down all the barriers and become a real goy. Worse than a goy. How could he have even entertained such craziness?

Indeed, he thought to himself as he set out to his lessons. *Indeed, I got muddled and started prattling on about God knows what. I very nearly promised to give up my lessons! But it doesn't matter. I made no contract with them. It'll just be a little uncomfortable when we meet—and really, I don't need to. So I won't go to Isser for tea. No great loss. They won't actually force me to return to the fold. And if they do anything bad to me, I can always go to the police superintendent, and he'll know how to handle them.*

Thinking about the superintendent now, Itzkowitz decided to drop in on him. He wanted to hear once again the superintendent's promise to defend him. And it was certainly more useful to spend time with the superintendent than with Isser. *There, at any rate,* he thought, *I get to hear and practice my Russian.*

That evening at the lesson, Yosel reminded him about yesterday's visit to Isser's and tried to invite Itzkowitz again, this time to Michoel's for tea. But Itzkowitz cut him off drily: "All that talk yesterday, it's all fine and good, okay for chitchatting over a drink . . . in the meantime, I'm a tutor. I can't make it to Michoel. I don't have time." And soon after the lesson, he left.

The next day, Friday morning, Itzkowitz went to the superintendent. On Fridays, Itzkowitz had no lessons scheduled because both parents and children were extremely busy preparing for Shabbos. Besides, on Friday it would be impossible to give evening lessons because it would already be Shabbos by then.

Itzkowitz found the superintendent in the office, along with a writer and the recently hired priest—a short, corpulent man with kind eyes and a somewhat grey beard.

The superintendent was surprised to see Itzkowitz so soon, but he welcomed him affably. "Ah! Mr. Tutor! What a pleasure," he said, remaining in his chair and extending his hand in greeting. "Here, Father, I have the honor to introduce you to the enlightener of Jewish youth. He deserves our love and respect."

"Very pleased to meet you, very pleased," the priest said, raising himself slightly. He brought his hand out from underneath his frock and extended it to Itzkowitz.

"He's a highly educated man, without superstitions," the superintendent continued to praise Itzkowitz. "Have a seat. Would you like some tea?"

"Thank you," Itzkowitz replied, sitting down.

"What's new? How're your business deals going? The rabbi hasn't excommunicated you yet, has he? Hasn't put you under cherem?"

"Heh heh. Cherem." His use of the Yiddish word encouraged Itzkowitz. "No, not yet. No excommunication so far. But the melamdim, they're fuming. It's frightful!"

"They're fuming? Well, just let them dare do something bad to you, and I'll teach them! See, that's how it is, Father, that's the sort of people they are! They're as afraid of education as the devil is of incense."

"They walk in darkness . . . a lost and stubborn people," the priest said, sighing. "Because of their hardheadedness, God punished them. He drove them out of their land and scattered them to the ends of the earth . . . But, excuse me, do you have a lot of students?"

"Eighteen."

"Do you mean you have a school?"

"No. I just give lessons. I go to them," the tutor answered laconically.

"Very nice. Very good."

"In my opinion, Father, it's not merely nice, it's a joy! Just think about it! They're not even decent human beings. With those fringed garments of theirs, they scream and yell and make a racket, and they don't understand a word of Russian! And just try and argue with them! But if they learn a bit of grammar, they'll soon become different people. Maybe they'll even become more devout. That's why I'm not even asking the tutor if he has a permit to teach. I'm not looking; it's slipping through my fingers. Like this." He placed the spread fingers of his hands on his face and peeked through them.

"God is good, God is benevolent," the priest murmured, sighing and shaking his head. "But you see, Fedor Stepanich, in my opinion, education won't improve the Jews."

"Why?"

"Because they're stubbornly defiant. As long as the light of Christianity's teachings doesn't light their way, they will not improve."

"It's possible," the superintendent almost agreed, then suddenly cried out vivaciously, "but perhaps, Father, we should have a little sip of something?"

"Well, that might help, I think, and certainly won't do any harm," the priest replied vaguely, raising his pointer finger high.

"As it is written: 'And drinking gladdens the heart,'" the superintendent affirmed in the same tone. "Grigoryev, hand us the flask in the closet," he said to the writer.

The priest finished his first glass and then, wiping his whiskers, he said to Itzkowitz, "You're an educated man, on balance. You've already passed all your exams and have immersed yourself in your studies: in physics, all kinds of sciences, and many other sorts of knowledge . . . So have you, would you say, already rid yourself of all Jewish superstitions?"

"He's eaten pork, Father. Pork!" the superintendent cried out. "What more do you need? For them, that's the original sin, so to speak. Excommunication!"

"You don't say. That means you've washed your hands of their prejudices because your eyes have been opened," the priest continued. "And yet, again you stand at a crossroads. If you *have* comprehended the truth, accept it! What's keeping you, Mr. Tutor, from throwing off the old and stepping into the lap of the Christian church?"

"Right," the superintendent cried, banging his fist on the table. "Upon my word! That's the absolute truth! What do you care anymore about your Itziks, your Yisroels? They've kicked you out, haven't they? Well, then, kick *them* away. Get yourself baptized! Because the way things stand right now, it's true, you're standing in the middle: neither here nor there; not for your soul, not for the devil!"

And without waiting for a response, he said with determination, "Indeed, Father, he'll be baptized, he'll certainly be baptized. He's already, even now . . . Look at him. Does he resemble some Baruch? He doesn't have a Jewish face at all. Upon my word!"

Itzkowitz, uneasy about the direction the conversation had taken, sat, his face pale and apprehensive, and looked about him helplessly.

The superintendent paced back and forth across the room a few times; then he walked over to Itzkowitz, placed his hands on his shoulder, and said genially,

"Eh, eh, young man. If you convert, you can be happy. Just think about the way you're living now. Everyone looks at you as upon a wolf; they'd happily kill you. But if you convert, you'll live like a count!"

"Last year someone, a young Jew from Nikola-yevka, converted," the writer said hesitantly, clearing his throat. "His godparents were the district chief of police, Ivan Micholovich Muraviov, and his wife. . . . And what do you think happened? Ivan Micholovich now considers him his own flesh and blood. He left him his house in his will and he found him a rich bride. Now the former Jew is a proprietor of an iron shop."

Itzkowitz felt he had to say something, anything. But he was so terrified and befuddled that he could not utter a word.

"I . . . I . . . I'm not a fanatic. I do everything . . . everything . . . ," he said in a quivering voice. "But to convert to Christianity, that I can't do. That I can't do. No!" he added, looking at the superintendent with a pleading look in his eyes.

"Why can't you? Do you believe your faith is better than the Christian faith? As an educated man—" the superintendent began.

"An old father, I have . . . very old . . . very devout, terrible! If I convert, he will die," Itzkowitz stammered.

"Therein lies the mistake!" the priest censured him. "Our Father who art in heaven comes before a person's earthly father. It is written, 'Leave your father and mother and follow me.' Have you read the Gospel?"

Itzkowitz, who was hearing this word for the first time, stared, dumbfounded, at the priest.

"Well, then, so you haven't read it? An educated person and he hasn't read the New Testament?" the superintendent wondered aloud.

"Give him the New Testament, Fedor Stepanich. Let him read it and contemplate it. God's light will fall upon him, too."

Now the superintendent was in a quandary. "I think that I don't . . ." the superintendent began, but then hastily caught himself. "Wait, what am I saying? I *do* have one!" And, quickly locating his New Testament, he handed it to Itzkowitz. "Take it. Read it, and mull it over, and then we'll talk," the superintendent advised.

"I'll read it," Itzkowitz replied obediently, timidly, and then said his good-byes.

He left the superintendent's place and ran, almost as if a phantom were pursuing him. He was petrified. It seemed to him that he'd been a hair's breadth away from being baptized by them. After all, the superintendent and the priest were no Isser and Yosel. With the latter he could argue, but if the priest and the superintendent were to force him to convert, what would he be able to do? Nothing! He was completely at their mercy.

He hid the New Testament deep inside his coat's breast pocket. He didn't know for certain what kind of book it was, but he figured it must have a direct connection to baptism. And that made him very anxious.

Oh, why did I go to the superintendent? But could he have known that he'd find the priest there and that this kind of conversation would ensue? On the contrary, he'd been expecting to again be praised for his activities and again be given the promise of protection, which had actually become necessary now after his confrontation with Isser and company. Instead, he'd had another confrontation, an even worse one, a more terrifying one—from the frying pan into the fire.

He didn't notice that he'd already reached the outskirts of town. Orchards stretched along both sides of the road. A bit farther down, they gave way to dense woods—the only area where the youth of Miloslavka could take a stroll.

Itzkowitz went into the woods. He wanted to be alone to ponder his current situation. In the woods, deathly stillness reigned; not a single living creature was visible across the path. The stroll calmed Itzkowitz. And truly, why should he be frightened? His fear was unfounded: he was in no danger. They were trying to persuade him, but no one would force him—neither to study the Gemara, nor to undergo baptism. All that had to be done was to remain steadfast and evade the persuaders, both the former and the latter.

The terror that had prevailed over him earlier during the conversation with the priest now gradually passed. And like lightning, the time it took to blink, this thought actually flashed through his mind: *And what if I were to actually convert? I'm not a Jew anymore anyway, I'm even worse than a convert* . . . Oh, what a clamor Isser and the entire town would raise! Itzkowitz couldn't help but smile. After a while, though, he told himself, *nonsense!* and began to think about something else.

He took stock of his current circumstances. He'd settled in quite nicely, he thought. He had enough food to eat and would even be able to save a bit of money.

He'd simply have to conduct himself a little differently: value his time, refrain from visiting Isser, be strict with Yosel.

His mood lightened, he felt a fresh surge of vitality rising in him, and lighthearted, with his head in the air, he turned toward home.

As soon as he stepped out of the woods, he saw a female figure coming from town, walking toward him. He recognized the figure immediately—Esther Dvoshe. He remained rooted to his spot, heart hammering. The prospect of meeting this girl here in the woods—this girl with whom he had such a strange relationship—both elated and scared him. Even during their lesson, with Esther Dvoshe's elderly mother a constant presence in the room, the proximity and wild passion of this girl excited him terribly.

Ten steps away from the tutor, the girl paused. Pretending that she'd just now noticed him, she emitted an artificial little laugh. "Ha! A chance encounter. And what a nice encounter! Here I am just taking a stroll and I chance upon you! What brings you here?" And she laughed in that affected way again.

She was, of course, hoping to fool him into believing that this encounter was a coincidence, to hide the truth of how she'd seen him going into the woods and had stood waiting for him to come out. When she could no longer stand to wait, however, she'd begun to walk toward the woods to meet him.

"I went for a stroll, too," Itzkowitz replied, his voice choked by excitement.

"For a stroll? Ha! Girls go strolling in the woods, not men. All the girls go strolling on Shabbos, but I can allow myself to go on Friday, also. I have nothing else to do."

Through passion-blurred eyes, she gave Itzkowitz a look. She said, "Well, do you want to take a stroll with a young lady? It's not a sin, is it?" and laughed.

"I don't consider it a sin," Itzkowitz replied, and moved very close to her.

They went into the woods and walked for several minutes without saying a word, their hearts beating wildly. Esther Dvoshe paused, and, not looking at Itzkowitz, she murmured, "Are you . . . not afraid . . . to walk . . . holding hands with a girl?" She didn't wait for a response. She snaked her arm through his and pressed herself against him.

The girl's touch scorched Itzkowitz. He did not look into Esther Dvoshe's face, but he saw the quick heaving of her breasts, he heard her rapid breathing, and he too felt breathless and dizzy. He held onto her hand, hugged her tightly, and whispered with fierce ardor, "I want to tell you . . . I . . ." He could not finish the phrase. But Esther Dvoshe understood him and completely powerless, she fell onto his arm. He held her firmly round her neck and kissed her on her cheek. Then, frightened at his boldness, he jumped backward, trembling. But the girl continued to hold tightly onto his arm and in a fervent, barely audible whisper, she said, "Come . . . there . . . in the woods . . ." And pulled him along with her.

20

Itzkowitz left the woods in a terrible mental state: depressed, a wreck, as if an avalanche had tumbled onto him and crushed him. He was afraid to venture back into town, afraid to see people. It seemed to him that anyone he met would be able to see on his face his depravity, his crime. And they'd all pelt him with stones.

Cautiously, unnoticed by his hosts, he tiptoed upstairs to his attic room, flung himself upon the divan, buried his face in his pillow, and burst into hysterical tears, murmuring repeatedly, "What have I done? What have I done?"

For a long time he lay like that, unconscious, thinking nothing, his mood as heavy as lead. It seemed to him that all was over and done with now. After what had happened, he could no longer show his face on the street.

It grew dark. It was already time to go to the synagogue. Then, dinner at home. Mustering tremendous willpower, he crept downstairs—exhausted, defeated—and, avoiding everyone's eyes, he muttered that he was feeling a bit ill and would therefore not go to the synagogue. He barely managed to sit through dinner. Only when he was alone in his room again did he relax somewhat. He got into bed right away, but couldn't fall asleep all night. He tossed feverishly, leaping out of bed again and again, his heart pounding. In front of his eyes danced the image of Esther Dvoshe, her enflamed face, her loose blond hair, her rapidly heaving breasts. And hardly had he managed to divert his thoughts that a new vision appeared: he saw himself plummeting from a great height into an abyss, and woke up screaming, drenched in cold sweat. Only at dawn did he finally fall into a deep sleep. When he awoke, he instantly remembered what had occurred and once again he was filled with dread and despair. It was, however, necessary for him to go to the synagogue. Not to go would draw too much attention to him. And so, gathering his strength, he left for the synagogue.

He'd imagined that as he walked down the street, fingers would be pointing at him. He imagined the epithet—Lecher!—and thought he already heard people shouting it at him. But all this was only in his imagination. A few old Jewish men and women, late to prayers and rushing toward the synagogue, greeted him. At the entrance to the synagogue, he bumped into Esther Dvoshe's mother. The old woman was happy to see him and nodded at him pleasantly.

"I thought I was the only one who was late," she said. "Turns out, you are, too."

This encounter, in particular, calmed Itzkowitz. It gave him the chance to consider the possibility that nobody would find out about his "depravity." Esther Dvoshe certainly wouldn't divulge it.

But when he stepped into the synagogue and was met with so many conspicuous glances, a deep sense of anxiety took hold of him again. It seemed to him that people were looking specifically at him, as if they were testing him, as if they knew something about him. Perhaps they'd found out he'd eaten pork at the superintendent's. Perhaps some of his other sins had been discovered. He was especially bothered by Isser's unnatural expression. His heart thumping madly and prepared for the worst, Itzkowitz picked up his prayer book and began to pray diligently.

Before the Torah scrolls were taken out of the ark, Itzkowitz noticed Gershon the beadle coming directly toward him. His heart withered. It seemed the synagogue had gone silent in anticipation.

"Reb Zalmen," Gershon said respectfully.

It's starting, Itzkowitz thought, and felt as if he were plummeting into a chasm.

"Reb Zalmen! The sexton has called you up to the Torah."

"Wait. This is none of your business," Isser interrupted, coming over. "I'm the one who's giving away my usual honor to Zalmen today, the honor of being the last to read from the Torah." Slapping Itzkowitz on the shoulder as one does to a friend, he added with a little smile, "See? I'm giving you the tastiest morsel— taking it right out of my mouth and giving it to you. But make sure not to embarrass me, okay? Everyone will be curious to hear your reading, of course."

"Take it easy. I'll do it no worse than anyone else," Itzkowitz assured him.

In truth, he had a knack for this. Back in yeshiva, before he'd become a Maskil, Torah readings were a sort of sport for the yeshiva boys, and Itzkowitz, who had a good voice, was always the winner.

Isser, still at Itzkowitz's side, seemed to be waiting for something. He looked toward the eastern wall, where the most respectable householders sat. Itzkowitz glanced in that direction and saw that something was happening there, a consultation of sorts, with people throwing inquisitive glances at him through it all. Finally, a sixteen-year-old boy, a cousin of the town's rabbi, stepped away from the group and walked over to Itzkowitz.

"The rabbi is asking for you," he told Itzkowitz.

"The rabbi?" Itzkowitz asked, shaky, apprehensive, and he glanced at Isser with a pitiful, pleading expression.

"Why are you so scared of the rabbi?" Isser asked suspiciously. "He won't eat you. If he's calling you, go."

Itzkowitz became befuddled. *Something's not quite kosher here*, he thought, and pale, dazed, with trembling legs, he went over to him.

His head covered with a tallis, the rabbi—a slight, gaunt old man with a sparse grey beard and sad, fatigued eyes—received Itzkowitz with a penetrating, cheerless glance. The men moved off to the side.

"Sholem Aleichem," the rabbi said serenely, extending a skinny hand from beneath his tallis.

"Hello to you, too, Rabbi," Itzkowitz replied, sounding lost.

"What's your name?"

"Zalmen."

"Whose son are you? Who's your father?"

"My father was a beadle."

"Where're you from?"

"Vitebsk."

"You studied in a yeshiva?"

"I did," Itzkowitz whispered, and sighed.

The rabbi's lips twitched, his cheerless eyes never leaving Itzkowitz's face. After a moment of silence, he said, "I heard you're a decent young man. I want to get to know you, talk with you. Come to me before the meal; today, you'll eat at my table."

Astounded by this unexpected honor, Itzkowitz became flustered, but recovering somewhat, he thanked the rabbi warmly.

"I heard you're quite a scholar," the rabbi continued. "I was told that you . . . you're not such a . . . anyway, we'll talk during the meal. So you'll come, won't you, my son?"

The rabbi said these last words in a particularly tender tone, and he gave Itzkowitz a good-natured glance.

Itzkowitz was about to respond, but just at that moment, people were starting to be called up to read from the Torah, and he swiftly went back to his place.

Now, it all became clear to Itzkowitz. The people's oppressive stares, the honor of reading the maftir, and the rabbi's invitation—all were related, all part of the offensive launched by Isser and company. They'd get him to come to the rabbi's house and then coax him back onto a path of piety. That's what this was all about! But this offensive not only didn't scare him;

on the contrary, it elated him. Let them attack! He wouldn't, of course, surrender. No, with smarts and shrewdness, he'd continue along his own path. At the rabbi's house he'd pretend to be a sincere, devout young man, but each time they'd make a concrete suggestion, he'd avoid giving a definitive answer. He would figure out how to deal . . .

Soon he would have to read the maftir, he remembered, and began to prepare for it. He was in excellent spirits; somehow, he felt as if he'd just survived some sort of mortal danger.

When he was called up to read, he boldly strode up to the reading desk, read the blessings clearly and precisely, and then began. He broke into soft, heartfelt song. The sad, dreamy melody stretched like one long infinite note, a bit higher here, a bit lower there; at its crux: a serene, tender prayer that made its listeners' breaths catch. Then, the melody trailed off into thin, barely audible vibratos.

The congregants, who earlier had gathered around the reading desk with skeptical smiles on their lips, soon stopped smiling. Captivated by the delicate melody, they looked at each other, astonished, as if to ask, "where did this come from?"

When he finished chanting, Itzkowitz stepped away from the reading desk like an artist after a successful debut. Proudly, he glanced about him, and in his demeanor was the question: *Well, then, do you get it now? Do you understand who it is you have in your midst?*

The congregants gathered round him and praised his voice and articulation. They'd never heard a maftir like this!

Languidly, Isser made his way over to Itzkowitz. With the air of one who is a great authority, he nodded his head and said with great earnestness, "Nice. Very nice!"

After prayers, Itzkowitz said to Leivik, "I won't be coming home for the midday meal. The rabbi invited me to his home."

"Yes, I heard about it," Leivik said.

Itzkowitz went over to the circle of men who'd gathered around the rabbi, and along with another smaller group, among whom were Isser and Yosel, he made his way to the rabbi's house. Once there, the rabbi's wife, the rebbetzin, a small, plump woman with a cheerful demeanor, welcomed him and greatly lauded his maftir.

"I'd give who knows what to hear such a reading every Shabbos."

"Eh, eh, Rebbetzin," Isser said with a faux-offended smile. "So that means my reading doesn't please you? Good to know! That's the end of our friendship."

"Oh, go away, you spoiled brat!" the rebbetzin replied, jovially giving him a slap on his shoulder.

When the visitors left, the others sat down at the table: the rabbi, his wife, their daughter and her husband, two grandchildren and two Shabbos guests. The rabbi seated Itzkowitz next to him, and the rebbetzin served him larger portions, as to an honored guest.

His success in the synagogue, the rabbi's wife's special attention, this sparkling room in a traditional Jewish environment that evoked memories of his childhood, the delectable filling meal—all of this put Itzkowitz in a festive mood.

After the meal, the rabbi was feeling cheerful: he joked with the kids and offered up a few common Gemara interpretations. Instead of reeling off entire interpretations, he uttered the first few words and then glanced at Itzkowitz, indicating that he should conclude it. Itzkowitz did so willingly. Afterwards, the rabbi's wife questioned him about his parents. When she found out he had lost both his father and mother, she cried "poor thing!" with such heartfelt warmth, such tenderness and love, that it conjured up in Itzkowitz the recollection, so long forgotten, of his mother's caresses. He felt a true sense of love and gratitude toward her.

The rabbi didn't lie down for a nap as he usually did, but instead called Itzkowitz into his room—a small room furnished with a table crammed with sacred texts and manuscripts, two bookcases, a regular chair and armchair, and a rather small bed, almost child-sized. On the wall hung a tallis sack that held a tallis and tefillin.

"Sit, my son, and we'll talk a bit," the rabbi said, as he himself sat down. Itzkowitz sat down next to him. He knew exactly what they were going to talk about, but he wasn't worried in the least. He felt love for the little old rabbi, and trusted him. A desire to cling to him with all his soul rose up in him, and he was prepared to obey completely whatever he would decree.

For a long time the rabbi sat silently, engrossed in his thoughts, his expression meditative and sad. Then he sighed deeply and began to speak in a low, unhurried, gentle tone of voice: "Listen, my son, to what I'm about to tell you . . . I was told you're a quiet type, a God-fearing young man, and I can see it's true. Now I want to discuss something with you seriously, with an open heart, like father to son, teacher to student, like a Jew with other Jews. Where are you going, son of mine? You abandoned the holy Torah and took upon you something that leads right to the abyss. Our sages said, 'Leave her for one day, and she'll leave you for two.' And now, many, many days have passed since you left her—our great and holy Torah—and where, on what kind of path, have you embarked? Just think about it. And remember. You became engrossed in secular wisdoms, you tarnished your thoughts and your heart with non-kosher books, and in your heart seeds of doubt may have fallen . . . but all you have to do is open your eyes to see the truth. Hundreds and thousands of the wisest men throughout the ages have studied our Torah, and written commentary on it. Is it possible they knew less, understood less, than the worldly wise from the other nations, than people with dull minds and hearts closed to God's commandments? Is it possible that a few insolent young men, whose faces have lost every shred of Godliness, who've lost every shred of self-restraint . . . is it possible that these people who've shamelessly forgotten and deny God and his Torah . . . is it possible that they, with their heretical and sinful books, can pit themselves against our great and holy sages?"

The rabbi gave a deep sigh, caught his breath, and continued, "You've abandoned the Torah, left her for secular wisdoms. That was your first step. Then you made a second move, this one even more terrible and sinful—*averah goreret averah*, one sin leads to the next: you discarded your Jewish appearance. You dressed like a German, snipped off your sidelocks. You became a 'writer' and began to teach our little Jewish children the sorts of things that contaminate the soul and dull the brain, that arouse all kinds of evil thoughts in the hearts of men. Just think about the kind of sin you're taking upon yourself! The sin of Jeroboam, son of Nebat, who sinned and compelled others to sin! You're sowing debauchery and depravity. The children you're teaching will become goyim; they'll speak Russian, forget their Jewishness and their God. A feud will grow; a struggle. My son! Don't you know the many difficulties the nation of Israel must endure here in exile: constant expulsions, constant libels. God punishes his chosen nation. But as long as we endure these things from strangers, it's not so terrible. What will be terrible, though, is when it comes from among our own, when those Jews who stand in the way and lead others astray will rise up like a plague that spreads to the very root.

"Listen, my son," the rabbi continued, his voice stronger now. "I beg of you, I implore you, as a rabbi I am ordering you—return! Shed all your impurities in a single moment. Break your will and return to God, to His Torah, and to Judaism! Have pity on yourself, have pity on your father and mother who are suffering because of you, poor things, in the afterlife, in the world of truth. Because of you, the doors of paradise are closed to them. Have pity on your poor, miserable nation of Israel, and return. Return to God *bechol leva-vecha uvchol nafshecha uvchol meodecha*,[1] with all your heart, all your soul, and all your fortunes. And God will forgive you for your sins. You already know He's a God of mercy and that every person who returns with all his heart is dear to Him."

The rabbi emitted a little whimper and became quiet, his head drooping as if all his strength had left him.

Itzkowitz had known in advance what the rabbi intended to discuss with him. So he'd listened a bit distractedly at the beginning, as he considered how to respond. He would start by complaining about the dean of his yeshiva, relate all he'd suffered from him, explain that he, Zalmen, was not only not "enlightened," but quite the reverse: the reason he was learning secular wisdoms was to be able to better refute the enlightened, to be able to present his viewpoint. But the more he listened to the rabbi's words, the more they moved him. He realized that this time it was inappropriate to come up with excuses. The rabbi's words touched the hidden nooks of his soul, touched its sorest tendons. All his grievances of this past year rose up in his mind, and he thought about how he'd lived, examining his life strictly and objectively. He listened to his inner voice, to what his muffled conscience was telling him,

---

1. Deuteronomy 6:5. This verse is a common part of an Orthodox Jew's lexicon, because it is found in the Shema prayer that is recited twice a day.

and a fear rippled through him. He had truly sunk into mire, hadn't paused to reflect, hadn't fought—for no particular reason, mere decadence. Indeed, was it possible that "they" knew more? All these scamps, these gymnasium students, "enlightened" babblers, complete ignoramuses of Torah—was it possible they understood more than old, esteemed people like this elderly rabbi, than hundreds and thousands of eminent Talmudic scholars, the greats of Judaism?

Haskalah! Enlightenment! What was this very renowned Haskalah comprised of? Wasn't it a child's game, sheer silliness? Grammar! The depths! Anarchy! Where was the deep wisdom that could compare to the Talmud?

And then there swam up in his consciousness latent grievances over insults he'd endured from various Maskilim. Had they ever acted toward him with such warmth, such tenderness, as this little old rabbi? Had they ever, those rich and well-fed Maskilim, wanted to know or acknowledge that he was suffering from hunger and cold? That he was torn and tattered? No, they'd throw a few groschen his way, as to a beggar, just enough for him not to die of starvation.

And he had gone and followed them, committed one sin after the other, tarnished his soul, plummeted into the abyss.

Gradually, a feeling of regret gathered in Itzkowitz's heart, a thirst to return, to cleanse himself. Something that had been pressing inside him, a pain, rose like a wave and stuck in his throat. "Rabbi! Tell me, teach me what to do! I . . . I'll do everything, whatever you tell me to do," he said in a choked voice.

"You yourself know what to do, my son," the rabbi said. "Return to God, abandon your studies, become a Jew, as you were before."

Itzkowitz got up and wanted to say something, but tears silenced him and he couldn't speak. He burst into a fit of weeping. "Rabbi," he finally cried, his voice broken, full of pleading and regret. "Rabbi, I'm a sinner. I'm full of sin. I'm not worthy of being called your son. I've transgressed all the commandments . . . I . . . I . . . Rabbi! I'm not at fault. I swear to you. They persuaded me, they duped me. That group of enlightened ones. They forced me. Rabbi! I give you my word. I swear by my portion of the world to come that I'll become a religious Jew again, that I regret my actions. From the depths of my heart, I regret. I'm ready to accept penance, anything you want to order me to do. Rabbi!" And he burst into loud sobs.

Deeply moved and nearly in tears himself, the rabbi whispered in a shaky voice, "God of Abraham, Isaac, and Jacob should strengthen your heart and point you toward the correct and true path." Then he hugged Itzkowitz and kissed him.

Itzkowitz fell upon the rabbi's gaunt, wrinkled cheek and kissed him at some length. Everything he said was accompanied with a pitiful sigh: "Rabbi. Rabbi."

The rabbi also spoke quietly through his tears. "Praised be your holy name. You have returned a Jewish soul to the path of righteousness."

Into the room came the rebbetzin.

"Kreina, we have a great God," the rabbi said to her in a celebratory tone. "Zalmen isn't a tutor anymore. He has returned to a religious life."

"Mazel tov, my son," the rebbetzin said quietly, with emotion. She hugged Itzkowitz and planted a kiss on his head. When she calmed down somewhat, she informed the rabbi that people were waiting for him in the other room. At this, the two of them went out.

Itzkowitz remained alone in the dim room. He sat with bent head, and a broken heart full of regret. Yes, he acknowledged, he'd been a great sinner, a really great sinner. And now he had returned to God with all his heart and all his thoughts, shed all his dirt, the whole evil sorcery of the Haskalah. He strained to remember all his sinful acts: he'd eaten pork, blasphemed God, violated all the holy commandments. The sin he'd committed yesterday had also, after all, stemmed from his enlightenment. Now he could see what all that enlightenment had done to him.

With horror, he thought about all his prohibited books, about his friends, his students, and about Esther Dvoshe. They all drew together in his mind into one great stream of sin, and he slashed all of it out of him. To suppress the heavy feeling weighing on him, he picked up a Psalms from the table and began to recite its words, softly, in its traditional plaintive melody. He struggled to penetrate the essence of each word, imbuing them with all the regret he felt so ardently, and all his yearnings to become pure. He prayed and prayed, and tears flowed from his eyes.

21

Itzkowitz remained at the rabbi's house till evening. After havdalah, the blessing that signals the
end of Shabbos, several members of the rabbi's clos-
est circle came over—Isser, Michoel, and Yosel among
them. They entered in a merry, festive mood. With a
resounding mazel tov, they pressed Itzkowitz's hand
tightly, slapped him on his back, and flooded him with
praise and good wishes.

"Rebbetzin!" Isser cried out. "Where's the rebbetzin? What is she thinking? Where's the drink she
promised?"

"Wait, wait, you'll have your drink," the rebbetzin
said. "What, did you think otherwise? How do the
peasants say it: *Moritch*! A deal is closed with a drink!"

Drinks and nibbles were passed around. The rabbi
poured himself a small glass and made a toast. "May
we get to drink when Jews will once again rejoice.
L'chaim, my son, may we get to drink when you have
completely forgotten your past, when all evil is eradi-
cated from our midst. L'chaim!"

Michoel added his own wish: "May we deserve to
drink when Zalmen receives rabbinical ordination."

"May we deserve to drink when Vilna burns down to its foundation," Isser cried.

"Shh," Michoel stopped him, "you forgot that those Vilna freethinkers have insurance on their homes. They'll actually be happy."

Mirthful, lively chitchat ensued. Everyone spoke at once. Isser no longer felt abashed: he revealed his cards, related how he and Yosel had diplomatically and shrewdly handled Itzkowitz.

"But I was the first one to say he'd retained his Jewish spark," Yosel bragged.

"Pure fabrication!" Isser interrupted him. "I was the first to say he's not yet completely ruined."

"Isser, you have a short memory," Yosel insisted. "You're forgetting you were planning to beat him up."

"I said that only on the condition of his being insolent—then I'd even be ready to give him a few slaps. But I saw right away that he was one of us. I asked him, 'What? You couldn't find a better job than tutoring?' And he answered me, 'What could I find?' Then he quoted the Gemara: 'Man should skin carcasses in the market rather than resort to the charity of other men.' A Jewish answer, isn't that so, Rabbi? A heretic or insolent person would never answer this way."

"I didn't actually say that, but it doesn't matter," Itzkowitz, who'd been feeling like a bridegroom through all of this, said, smiling.

When everyone had calmed down a bit, they began to figure out how to deal with the issue practically.

"First of all, you must look like a Jew," Michoel said to Itzkowitz. "You'll get rid of the short jacket, the white shirtfront; you'll shave and leave sidelocks."

"No, first he must go to the ritual bath," Isser said. "He must submerge, as is proper."

"I'll tell Gedalye the attendant to heat up the bath tomorrow," Yosel interposed.

"The first thing you must do, my child," said the rabbi, "is to clear out all your impurities. The books . . . they must go first. Bring them here tomorrow and throw them into the furnace. Let them go up in smoke."

"Of course, I'd already thought about doing that," Itzkowitz answered weakly.

"But why should we bring all that impurity into your home, Rabbi?" Michoel said. "Best to take them to the bathhouse and burn the whole lot all at once: the books, his shirtfront—the "white heart"—and the short jacket. None of it is worth a thing anyway," he said, laughing.

"Afterwards, my child, you'll spend your time studying Torah. No work, no worries. You'll be able to devote yourself to the Torah undisturbed. I myself will study *Poskim* with you a few hours every day, so that we can review Jewish law. We'll study the text, *Likutei Torah*, its weekly Torah portions. We'll see . . ."

"And what about his meals?" Yosel said. "We have to think about that, too."

"On Friday and Shabbos he'll eat at my house," the rabbi said.

"And on Tuesdays, at mine," Isser announced.

"I'll give him meals on Sundays and my brother Eli will certainly give Mondays," Michoel said.

"See, you already have five days covered," Isser told Itzkowitz. "I'm certain my father-in-law will give you that one other day. In short, as far as your livelihood, you're taken care of. You won't die of hunger."

The question about his meals reminded Itzkowitz of his overall financial situation, but he was embarrassed to talk about this in front of everyone. Drawing Isser aside, he reminded him that besides food, a person had other needs, too. A living human being had to use the bathhouse, have his shirt washed, his shoes fixed, smoke a cigarette, et cetera. Besides, he'd been eating at Chana Leah's for two weeks now and would have to pay her. Of course, he was still owed for the lessons he'd given, but the mothers would likely refuse to pay.

"Don't you worry about any of this," Isser interrupted him. "Everything will be taken care of. The mothers, no matter how reluctant, will have to pay. I'll send the beadle to them with a note. As for the money you owe, I'll work it out with Leivik. And concerning your expenses—how much do you need? A few kopecks, ten-kopecks a week, it's not even worth talking about. Just ask me, and I'll give it to you."

The last of Isser's promises reminded Itzkowitz of his past life of beggary, dependent on his fellow Maskilim for "a few kopecks," but he tried hard to smile and even thanked him politely.

When the guests were getting ready to leave, Isser—not entirely convinced of the sincerity of Itzkowitz's repentance—decided to avoid leaving him alone for now, and invited him to sleep at his house.

The next morning, Itzkowitz went to his lodgings to get his books and bring them to the bathhouse to be burned.

"But make it fast, don't dillydally," Isser said to him. "Don't forget I'm a busy man."

Itzkowitz walked to his lodgings in a somber mood, but he tried hard to think about nothing and just kept repeating to himself that it was all over now, and it was better this way, much better.

At the inn, he was about to tell Chana Leah what had occurred, but before he could say a word, she cried out, her happiness sounding fake, "I heard, I heard! The whole town's boiling like a kettle. Well, mazel tov! May we deserve . . ."

"Tell me, did I do the right thing?" Itzkowitz began, wanting some approval on the step he'd taken. "You saw it yourself, didn't you, that tutoring wasn't for me . . ."

"Of course, of course," Chana Leah cried out. "I kept thinking to myself all the time: Poor thing! A man like this. And here, of all places! But God be praised, at least you came to your senses!"

"What are they saying in town?"

"Do you really need to ask? What do you think? It's like a holiday in town! And actually, I wanted to ask you something. They say your father came to you in your dreams on three consecutive nights and exhorted you to repent . . . Is that true?"

"Oh, that's of no consequence! He came, he didn't come. It doesn't matter. As long as I made the firm decision that I've had enough of acting silly, being crazy . . . It's high time I started living like a mensch." Then he informed her that Isser would pay whatever he still owed her and went upstairs to get his stuff.

Itzkowitz had decided to take all the books he owned to be burned. But now, as he gathered them up, he felt overcome by a great sense of compassion. Here were these brand new books: textbooks on history and geography, which also introduced the sciences. Here was the grammar text—torn, pitiful, but what a little dear she was! Here was also the arithmetic text along with its workbook. How many dreams and plans these books were imbued with, how much soul they held! All his "worldly wisdom," all he'd lived for during the past year, was concentrated in these books as in a magnifying glass. And now, with his own hands, he'd have to extinguish this light, sever the connection between past and present?

His feelings grew even drearier when he picked up the Hebrew books to which so many memories were attached. His heart pressed painfully against his chest, and with his voice choking, as when one bids farewell to a beloved person on his deathbed, he managed to murmur, "Haskalah . . . Haskalah . . ."

All at once he recalled that beneath his divan, the New Testament lay hidden. Because of all the excitement, he'd completely forgotten about this book these last few days. The New Testament naturally reminded him of the superintendent and the priest—and a quiver went through his body. He opened it and began to read: "The birth of Jesus, son of David, son of Abraham . . ."

Immediately, from its opening words, he understood what kind of book he was holding in his hand. Yes, this was a book about Christianity, about baptism, a book forbidden in a Jewish home. What should he do with it? He couldn't even bring it to be burned, because if Isser or Yosel were to discover it, they'd be frightened to death. Anyway, how could he destroy a book that belonged to the superintendent? What would happen when the superintendent asked for it back?

He vacillated for a while and then decided he'd hide the book somewhere in the attic for the time being. Then a thought flashed through his mind: *I might as well hide the grammar text, too, right?*

The grammar text was his most beloved book, the hardest one to part with. So he decided to hide it, too. After all, the grammar book truly did not hold one iota of heresy inside it.

He found a corner in the attic where some bricks lay about, and industriously, he hid the grammar text and the other questionable book beneath the bricks. Wrapping the rest of the books in paper, he said with determination, "I'm taking these away! No need to be sparing with them. I have to bring an offering, do my penance."

He remembered suddenly that he'd lent one of his books—the most heretical one!—to Elya. And at the thought of Elya, a heavy, fearful feeling enveloped him. For a moment he thought about what to do with that book, but finally he made a gesture with his hand, as if waving it all away. *Let it be. I won't ask for it back. I wasn't the one to ruin him, and I won't flog myself for it.*

He arrived at Isser's house, holding his books and a package, and found Yosel and two other melamdim there.

"Pshaw! What a slowpoke!" Isser cried out, "We should send you to bring the angel of death . . . What were you doing there for so long? Here are clothes for you. Try them on. This is my jacket."

Isser handed him a long, dirty jacket, torn in places, and a soiled velvet hat. Itzkowitz tried them on. The jacket was too wide, too big. The hat, too, was big on him. He was about to say that the clothes were not his size at all, but Isser and Yosel cried out excitedly, "Perfect! As if tailor-made for you! Excellent. Look, he already looks completely different. A decent face! The jacket is a bit wide, but with God's help, you'll put on weight, and it'll fit just right!"

Itzkowitz did, however, get a quite new yarmulke. He picked up the bundle of clothes and his books, and along with Isser and a few others, left for the bathhouse.

22

For days now, rumors about the tutor's "repentance" had been circulating around town. When the Hebrew teachers were questioned, they replied brusquely, "Man's heart is in God's hands. Live long enough, and you'll find out. In the meantime, no need to talk."

Only Isser gave a different response. Harshly, with hostility in his tone, he said, "It'll all come to naught now. A fig's worth, that's what you'll get, not a tutor!"

The rabbi's invitation to Itzkowitz for his Shabbos meal had finally made the truth obvious to everyone. If there were no validity to the rumors of Itzkowitz's repentance, would the rabbi have invited him?

The town was bubbling. Once again, the tutor had become the hero of the day. Everywhere, they spoke only about him. Some said that Itzkowitz's dead father had visited him in his dreams and threatened to strangle him if he didn't repent. Others recounted that Itzkowitz's father came to the rabbi in a dream and begged him to save his son. Still others told another version: back when Itzkowitz had still been in the yeshiva, he'd been preparing to become a rabbi when a huge fight broke out between him and his yeshiva dean. As a result, he abandoned the proper Jewish path. Now, however, he'd received a letter from the dean, begging Itzkowitz to forgive him. And so, Itzkowitz had decided to return to the yeshiva.

Just as upon his arrival, now, too, the town was divided into two groups. The women whose children hadn't studied with Itzkowitz gloated triumphantly, thrilled that vengeance was theirs: "They all rushed into it! Didn't have enough time. Hurried as fast as they could to turn their children into goyim. Well! They got what was coming to them. Well deserved!"

"Who ended up being right?" preached one of the young shopkeepers who'd actually already been planning to hire Itzkowitz to tutor her daughter. "I said right away there was no need to rush . . ."

"No, what makes me happy is that Menachem Treines's wife, Tzirel, fell flat on her face! This'll beat the arrogance right out of her. Just recently, she was busy raising her expectations of the matches her daughters could make, because after all, they were becoming regular ambassadorettes. They were already capable of writing to the tune of thousands and tens of thousands of rubles—whole fortunes! Well, she's got herself a right fortune now!"

"I'm giving eighteen kopecks to charity in honor of Reb Meir Baal Haness," another one cried. "I already gave eighteen a while ago, asking for the tutor to suffer a horrible death. It's all the same. So *he* didn't get punished. But a few of these respectable mothers did!"

"True as I'm a Jewish daughter, I would kiss him all over. Now our conceited princesses will have something to remember. Hah! Now that's what I call a teacher. A real teacher! He taught them all some sense."

"You can so plainly see that we have a great God," one little old lady concluded.

Because of all this, the women whose children had studied with Itzkowitz were feeling defeated and humiliated. And because they could not come up with any justification for their actions, they each tried to shift the blame onto somebody else:

"It always has to be you!" Devorah Kazanov yelled at her husband. "It was really important, wasn't it, for you to be the first to jump in. No matter what I said, no matter how I pleaded with you, like with a thief, how I begged you not to rush—but no, you had to stick to your guns. Now you have what you wanted! Be happy! You made yourself into a fool in front of the whole town. We won't be able to lift our heads in front of people."

"May she be punished for talking me into it," Gnessa Yachnes said, cursing Menachem Treines's wife, Tzirel. "She said to me, 'If *I* sent my children to study, you can send your children, too.' You know how she is, that fat sow! Not enough that she herself crawls into the mud, she has to pull others along with her."

"What did I need this for?" Tzirel yelled furiously. "Chana Leah alone is to blame! That apostate! Let her go to hell! She unearthed this jewel, so let's bury her instead! She sent him to me; let's send her to the doctor! She spoke to me about him; let's now speak about her—in a eulogy! That's when I'll thank her for all this."

More than anyone else, Esther Dvoshe was in a state of terror. Desperately incensed, she cursed the tutor loudly, mouth frothing: "What a dog! What a bastard! And he deems himself a tutor? Let him show his face, and I'll spit on it!"

Itzkowitz's students—the boys and the girls— also had plenty to endure from their friends and parents. The former mocked them. "Tutor! Tutor!" they chanted, and stuck out their tongues. The latter unleashed all their anger at them, as if they were the ones chiefly at fault for this catastrophe. "Here you have it, you louts! Couldn't stop badgering: 'Study, study, we want to study!' And we should give them paper and ink and books and all kinds of madness. Well, now you have yourself a tutor!"

The real commotion began on Sunday, by which time everyone had learned the details of the "repentance," and had also heard that the tutor would be brought to the ritual bath that morning. Despite it being a market day, the streets teemed with clusters of people awaiting the procession. Isser, who'd been anticipating this, led Itzkowitz through roundabout side streets. But the crowd had already managed to gather at the bathhouse, too. Itzkowitz was met with loud shouts, mostly amiable ones. Isser, as the boss he considered himself to be, shouted back at the crowd and ordered the bathhouse attendant not to allow anyone inside.

In a corner of the large, dim, smoky bathhouse, lay a sort of pool of cloudy green water, which emitted the stench of a stagnant, putrefied swamp. In another corner, a pile of stones, reddened and glowing, were heating the bathhouse.

"The rabbi sent a message saying he's also coming," Gedalye, the bathhouse attendant informed them.

Soon, indeed, the rabbi arrived, accompanied by Gershon the beadle and other members of his entourage. "We have to finish this as quickly as possible," the rabbi said to the bathhouse attendant. "Gedalye, take the scissors."

Gedalye took a large scissors and began to cut Itzkowitz's hair. The scissors was blunt and Gedalye used it ineptly, though with great determination. Itzkowitz twisted, groaned, shook, and bobbed. After the uncomfortable operation, Itzkowitz's head was left covered in patches of hair and bald spots. A bit of hair left at the ears were to serve as his sidelocks.

Gedalye gathered up the cut hair and placed it aside.

"Rabbi, here are the books," Itzkowitz said, unwrapping a package.

Upon seeing *The Dawn*, the rabbi burst out agitatedly, "Terrible, terrible! What books!"

"Why are you holding them in your hands?" the rabbi said to Isser. "Let Gershon take them and . . ." He didn't complete the sentence, but Gershon understood. He took the books, sat down on the floor in a corner, and began to stack the books in a pyramid. He did this serenely, with concentration, like a child playing, constructing a house of cards. He tore some of the books into several pieces. Others, he tore off only the covers. He piled up the ripped books into a two-story edifice and observed the results of his work with satisfaction. Then he gathered up the cut hair, placed it on top, and lit a flame to all of it. Quite slowly, the pages caught fire, the flames gradually spreading through the entire house of cards. A thick smoke rose from it, and in minutes all the books had turned into a pile of smoldering ash, though some sparks still wove through the ash like snakes of fire.

"And so shall all evil toward the nation of Israel disappear along with the fire and smoke," the rabbi said.

Now came the second ceremony: the ritual immersion. With no small degree of embarrassment, Itzkowitz began to undress. He was ashamed of his dirty body, his torn shirt. Naked, he ran to the bath—gaunt, hunched, pitiful. His entire body quivering, he hurried down the steps into the water. He dunked three times and wanted to run back out, but the rabbi stopped him. Filling his hands with water, he poured it over Itzkowitz, saying unhurriedly and with fervor: "And I will spray you with pure water and you will become cleansed of all your sins and your paganism. I will make you flawless. And I will give you a new heart, and a new spirit will I bring into you. And I will remove the stony heart from your body and bestow upon you a heart of flesh. And my spirit will I bring inside you, and will make it so that you keep my laws and fulfill my commandments."

The entire crowd then echoed these Biblical verses.

When he left the bath, Itzkowitz put on his yarmulke first. Then he put on his "new" clothes. Everyone was duly impressed.

Comments flew from every direction: *A whole different face! A whole different person! A Jewish face!*

"Mazel tov, my son," the rabbi congratulated him. Mazel tov! Mazel tov!

Timidly, Gedalye asked Isser if he could give the short jacket as a gift to the gentile who heated the bath. After some hesitation, Isser agreed.

From the bath, Itzkowitz went to Michoel for lunch. Then, he went to his new quarters: the synagogue.

The synagogue was empty. Itzkowitz looked around as if trying to acquaint himself with his new home. Then he looked at his long jacket, stained with grease, and sighed deeply. He felt mentally and physically fatigued, exhausted, broken, and was glad to be finally alone. He needed to take stock of his situation, but his head felt heavy and all he could do, in his attempts to reassure himself, was murmur, "Good. Very good. It's better this way."

He lowered himself onto a bench and for a little while he sat this way, without moving, his head bent.

Right now I'd have been at the lesson with . . . Esther Dvoshe, he thought suddenly and jumped up from where he sat, trembling. *How lucky that it had ended this way! How would I have been able to go to her? How could I have looked into her eyes?* But then his thoughts veered in a different direction: *Who said she's that angry? Maybe . . . maybe she isn't . . .* But his sinful thoughts scared him, and to banish them, he opened a Gemara and began to study. His exhaustion won out, though, and he fell asleep.

Gershon woke him when the crowd was already beginning to arrive for the afternoon prayers. The worshippers went over to Itzkowitz with somber faces, extended their hands, and fervently congratulated him. He responded with equal fervor.

In the evening after supper at Michoel's, he returned to the synagogue. Only Gershon was there. At first, the beadle said nothing. Then he looked about him, and serenely, as if he were just uttering words addressed to no one, said, "It's warm here. Quiet. One can sit here all day and all night studying Torah. There's enough light in the closet . . ." He sighed. Itzkowitz sighed, too.

Gershon didn't feel like leaving yet. He stood quietly for a while and then initiated a conversation: "In Vitebsk they probably have a bigger synagogue than ours here, right? A nicer one?"

"No comparison! A palace!"

Gershon sat down on the bench next to Itzkowitz. Inclining his head, he asked, "Do you have a father? A mother?"

"No, I'm an orphan," Itzkowitz replied forlornly. With much emotion, he said, "My father was a beadle in a little town named L. A tiny town, smaller and poorer than Miloslavka. All his life my father was a beadle. I remember him well: old, sick, hunched over, nearly blind. Always coughing and moaning. The merchants would yell at him and he wouldn't say a word. He accepted his lot in life docilely, with love for God. As a boy, I was always hanging about the synagogue; sometimes I even slept there. I like synagogues."

"It's quiet. And somehow so melancholy," Gershon said.

"Yes, something like that."

"As if close to God," Gershon found the right words. "When I was still a little boy, I was afraid to stay in the synagogue alone. Even now, I don't like to stay here till very late. They say the dead come here at night to pray. They take out the Torah scroll and read . . ."

"Nonsense! The things people say! The Gemara says the dead are exempt from the obligation to pray."

"About five years ago," Gershon continued, "my son drowned. He was twelve years old. To this day, if I'm alone in the synagogue at night, I feel as if he's here, sitting in that dark corner. At home I never see him. But here I see him often, so clearly that I imagine I hear him breathing. I say a quiet Kaddish. Or I say, 'Little son, go and rest.' I say it three times, and it helps. He disappears." He breathed out deeply and rose from the bench. "Well, then, good night," Gershon finally said. "I'll come early in the morning and wake you."

Alone now, Itzkowitz paced back and forth across the synagogue a few times. He felt calmer than during the day. The overall stillness and the conversation with Gershon had relaxed him. *Well, I'm a yeshiva boy again,* he thought without an iota of bitterness. *Once again I'm in a long jacket, once again I'm in a synagogue, having my meals in different people's homes again, as if nothing has ever occurred in the interim. How strange man is, never knowing what the next day will bring. Could I have foreseen this would happen to me? It's almost as if it happened on its own. But why brood? It happened. It's done. And now I have to start acting like a mensch. We have to endure the worse times patiently, and then it'll be good. The townspeople won't abandon me. I'll become engaged to a girl; my life will find purpose.*

He thought: *I'll have to struggle to become a regular Jew. All year I played around, acted like a fool. Enough.*

Time to become devout again. It's not that hard, is it? It's quite easy. In fact, if you pray with fervor, your heart actually becomes lighter.

These thoughts calmed Itzkowitz completely. He took a bench near the stove as a bed for himself and was about to lie down when he suddenly noticed faces pressed against the windowpane, observing him with curious eyes.

"Bastards!" he yelled, hurtling toward the window. The faces instantly disappeared. "Peeking. Sniffing around. They have to know what I'm doing. As if it's their business!"

This small episode changed his mood entirely. He recalled his attic room and now deeply regretted having left it. "Not enough they exhaust me all day with their ritual bath and their other stupidities," he muttered furiously, "now they even have to know what I do at night? Do they want to know if I'm repenting properly? Lowlifes!"

The next morning, Itzkowitz was called to the Torah and he recited with fervor the blessing of Gomel giving thanks to God for His mercy.[1] After breakfast, he went to the rabbi, who had promised to study with him for a few hours each day. Itzkowitz wasn't completely at ease; he felt terrified, as before an exam.

In Miloslavka there was no yeshiva, and so the few young unmarried men who were studying and

1. The blessing of Gomel (*Birkat Ha-Gomel*) is the traditional prayer of thanks to God after one has survived a dangerous situation.

not yet working, usually studied at home and came to the rabbi when they had difficulty understanding something.

The rabbi greeted Itzkowitz warmly, invited him to have a seat, and said with some satisfaction, "So, I finally get a good student with whom it'll be a pleasure to study. Have you ever studied *Likutei Torah*?"

"As a matter of fact, no. But I know of it. Not insignificant, this *Likutei Torah*! It's profound! Boundless!" Itzkowitz managed to stammer.

"Well, let's give it a try." The rabbi opened the text and pushed it toward Itzkowitz. He leaned back in his chair and closed his eyes in concentration, prepared to listen.

Itzkowitz skimmed the first line and began to recite in the traditional learning tune.

The rabbi stopped him. "A bit lower. Without a tune."

Itzkowitz paused and started again, this time using the correct tone: not too loud, slow, dry, and matter of fact. He recited the words, placing the accent on the more important ones. The rabbi listened silently. After he recited an entire page up to the page break, the rabbi, eyes still closed, stopped him by holding up his finger and asked, "We-ell?"

Itzkowitz understood the rabbi was waiting for his gloss. But he couldn't grasp the essence of what he'd just read and so he again began to skim the page.

The rabbi opened his eyes and stared at Itzkowitz, surprised. "You didn't understand it?"

"No, I did . . . I understood."

"Explain it to me in two words."

Itzkowitz started to explain, but his words made no sense, and so he once again began to read the page and translated literally, word for word.

"But it's really easy," the rabbi cut him off, and in a few scant words, he explained it.

"Okay, now continue," the rabbi said. He no longer closed his eyes, but looked at the text together with Itzkowitz.

Itzkowitz, flushed and perplexed, continued hesitantly. The further along he got in the kabbalah lesson, the more difficult it became. In the end, he stopped trying to understand it and merely recited the words mechanically, senselessly, like a lost wanderer feeling in the dark.

"Leave it," the rabbi said impatiently, stopping him. "You're studying without thinking. Looks like you're not used to difficult topics. Whatever the case, *Likutei Torah* isn't for you. We'll try an ordinary passage of Gemara."

He opened a Gemara and instructed Itzkowitz to read it and explain the topic discussed. This tractate was familiar to Itzkowitz and he began to explain the page pretty well. But the rabbi, with the sensitivity of a deeply experienced Talmudist, immediately discerned that Itzkowitz had already studied this topic previously.

"Have you already looked over this tractate?" he asked cheerlessly.

"Yes . . . I have," Itzkowitz replied, not having the courage to lie.

The rabbi chose another tractate, one rarely studied in yeshivas, and told Itzkowitz to read through it and explain it. Itzkowitz, flushed from agitation, and befuddled, began to read it, stumbling over the words, pausing, stammering, not understanding the meaning of many of the words, not understanding the context. After ten minutes of this exhausting exercise, he became silent, beaten and humiliated.

For a long while afterwards, the rabbi sat without saying a word, his head bent, an expression of extreme disbelief on his face.

"No, my child," he said with a deep sigh, "I was mistaken about you. You still have to study a lot, with diligence and using your head. You study Gemara— forgive me—like a cheder boy, with no flavor . . . just to . . . seems like you've gotten out of the habit of working at it, figuring out the meaning . . . but, well, too bad." Again, he sighed. "Don't let it discourage you. We'll start on another tractate. Come to me tomorrow."

Itzkowitz understood how profoundly he'd been disgraced in the rabbi's eyes, and he left feeling crushed and disheartened.

That evening the rabbi met Isser. "You told me," the rabbi said, "that Zalmen was a great scholar, a man with a keen mind. Where'd you get that from?"

"Yosel told me."

"Yosel . . . Ha! You rely on Yosel's scholarliness!? Well, then, you should know he's still a long way from having a keen mind. He's dull-headed, without a glint of contemplativeness."

"What are you talking about, Rabbi?" Isser cried, astonished.

"I studied with him today. We started with *Likutei Torah*, but he didn't understand a thing. Then I gave him an ordinary page of Gemara, and it was so terrible to listen to the way he was learning it—like a cheder boy."

"Well, look at that! And here we thought we'd found a treasure."

"Whether he's a treasure or not, still better than if he'd remained a heretic."

The next morning after prayers, Itzkowitz went over to Isser to talk to him, but Isser cut him off curtly. "I don't have time," he said. Then he gave Itzkowitz a look of disdain and told him, "The rabbi told me you're not the greatest of scholars. In Vitebsk you were probably one of the average yeshiva boys, and now you've forgotten even what you knew then. How embarrassing!" And turning away rudely, he stalked off.

Itzkowitz remained standing in the middle of the synagogue as if someone had spit in his eye. Even worse, a few of the townsmen had heard the exchange.

In the evening Itzkowitz went to the rabbi and said hesitantly, "You see, Rabbi . . . this whole last year I haven't once held a Gemara in my hands, and so, of course I'm not used to it. As is written, 'If you leave her for one day, she will leave you for two.' I don't want to make you uncomfortable anymore, so I'd rather study on my own for a while. Once I work my way up, I'll come back to you."

"Good. But don't let it discourage you. Remember that the most important thing isn't study, but deeds, mitzvahs. May God help you," the rabbi said tenderly, trying to be encouraging.

But Itzkowitz understood quite well that, coming from him, these words were a final judgment.

23

For Itzkowitz, a new life had started. Or rather, his old life had *re*started, and he resumed living like a yeshiva boy: constant studying of the Gemara, always eating at strangers' tables. Once again, his old way of thinking with its petty, paltry interests and worries rose to the surface. And yet, there was something new to his current yeshiva-boy life, which Itzkowitz hadn't anticipated and which was now increasingly poisoning his life. In the yeshiva in Vitebsk, Itzkowitz was part of a circle of friends and acquaintances whom he trusted implicitly and with whom he shared his joys and sorrows. Here, however, he was completely alone, deserted. In Vitebsk, while he'd been a yeshiva boy, he'd felt he was in the right place, unaffected by being called a yeshiva boy as an insult or by his greasy pauper's clothing. The relationship between him and his environment was clearly established. Everyone bossed him around, and that made sense to him; he wasn't vexed by it at all. Neither did his ego suffer when he ate charity meals at strangers' tables. Now, however, it was entirely different. The awareness of his self-worth as an individual being had been roused inside him, albeit very weakly; he'd already tasted the bread he himself had earned, he'd already tried living independently. Now, everything chafed at him: Isser's abuse, the rude, coarse dealings of the women at whose homes he ate, and the very realization that he was a yeshiva boy. Besides all this, he was now burdened by the religious yoke of performing mitzvahs, to which he'd already become unaccustomed; by the necessity of studying all day; and in general, by the entire spiritual aspect of this new life. His clothes aggravated him tremendously. In the stranger's long, dirty coat and oversized hat and yarmulke, he felt as if he were wearing prisoners' garb. Whenever he passed through the market, he always heard someone laughing behind his back, but he was obliged to walk through the market a few times a day.

The relationship between Itzkowitz and the townspeople also wasn't good. How could they trust a tutor who'd returned to the fold after having left? So they viewed him with suspicion. Everyone wanted to pry, to crawl into his soul to know what he was thinking and feeling.

With each passing day, he felt worse than the day before. He became extremely depressed and severely neglected his appearance. He looked like a savage. The study of Gemara became more and more tedious. At night, once the fire fizzled out and he remained alone in the dark, he cried, burying his face in his pillow.

Three weeks passed.

One day, when Itzkowitz was alone in the synagogue, Elya entered. He stood at the door and for several minutes stared harshly and unyieldingly at the repentant tutor. At the sight of his former kindred spirit, Itzkowitz became disoriented. Over the last three weeks, he hadn't met up with Elya, and he realized that Elya had been avoiding him, too. Now, Elya was staring at him with animosity. Itzkowitz lowered his eyes, as if engrossed in the Gemara lying open in front of him. Elya walked over and stopped right next to Itzkowitz. In a fervent, rigid voice, he said, "I want to tell you everything I'm feeling in my soul. Until now, I thought you were doing all this skillful playacting in order to fool the rabbi and the Hebrew teachers. But now I see you actually rejected the entire Haskalah, your whole new life. You returned to the old, to the Gemara! That's why I want to tell you, I must tell you, that you . . . that you—" His voice caught and choked from his great agitation, but he soon regained control, and in a steely tone, without a shred of sympathy as if hurling a bloody insult, he concluded his sentence: "—that you are a Jeroboam, son of Nebat, a renegade and heretic of the Haskalah. And just like Jeroboam, you'll always be cursed!"

And he strode out of the synagogue.

Itzkowitz sat there, broken and crushed. He couldn't come up with a single word he might have said to defend himself. For a long time, he was frozen in place, his mind blank, as if the bitter reproof had forged him to this spot.

The next morning after prayers, Gershon approached him and said, "I met Chana Leah, and she told me a letter has arrived for you."

Itzkowitz startled. "For me? A letter? From who?"

"I don't know. Go get it from her."

Itzkowitz went to see his ex-landlady. She handed him a crumpled letter and said, "It's been here for a week already. I kept forgetting to send it over to you."

With trembling hands, Itzkowitz ripped open the envelope. The letter was from a friend in Vitebsk. His eyes glued to the densely written sheet of paper, Itzkowitz began to read:

Dear Friend,

I received your letter three weeks ago, but I haven't had time to respond. I've been poring over my textbooks all day and all night, working beyond my strength—and yesterday I finally passed the exams. Congratulate me! I'm already a sixth grade gymnasium student and feel like I'm in seventh heaven. I have a wide path ahead of me now, a wide open world—and I'm the happiest man in the world. Congratulations to you, too! I and all our friends were very happy at the news that you've settled in well and hope to accomplish much in the area of ___ well, you know what. You write that you had, and still have, a lot to fight against. Don't worry! Remember, he who sows with tears, reaps with song! Looks like you'll have a rich harvest. Mendel was envious of you when he read your letter. 'Itzkowitz,' he said, 'is happier than all of us: he's on the battlefield while we're only sharpening our weapons.' But be careful, and remember that you're dealing with wolves who'll tear you to pieces if they find out about your past and your goals. Work quietly and diligently. With a generous hand, strew the seeds of the holy Haskalah into young hearts. If you need books, we can send them to you, but to a safe address only; otherwise, our project will fail.

Don't worry, brother, don't lose courage! Remember that you're not alone, that hundreds and thousands of other Maskilim are quietly doing the same holy work you are: preparing the soil for this new life to take root.

Itzkowitz reread the letter and felt faint. Ashen, with tears in his eyes, he collapsed onto a chair.

"What's the matter with you?" Chana Leah cried, frightened. "Did you get bad news?"

"Yes," Itzkowitz barely managed to reply.

"What exactly? Is someone sick?"

"No, dead . . . my best friend," Itzkowitz said, meaning himself.

"Blessed be the true judge," Chana Leah said, invoking the blessing said upon hearing of someone's death. "What a tragedy! A young man? What did he die of?"

"He drowned himself," he answered in a dead voice, and continued to gaze blankly into space.

"Ay, the kinds of tragedies that happen in this world!" Chana Leah said. "I completely forgot, did you hear about the tragedy that struck Chaya and Shmiel?"

"What happened?" Itzkowitz asked, indifferently.

"A son of theirs, a seventeen-year-old, disappeared. Yesterday, sometime in the middle of the day, he left, no one knows where. By suppertime, in the evening, he hadn't returned. He didn't come home to sleep, either. He's still not here, disappeared like a stone in water."

"Whose son, did you say?" Itzkowitz asked.

"Shmiel and Chaya's, the tavern owner. You must have seen him in the synagogue. A skinny boy, refined."

"Wears an astrakhan hat?"

"Yes, yes."

"His father lives not far from Gnessa-Yachne's?"

"Yes, yes."

Itzkowitz realized that the missing boy was Elya, who had cursed him with intense bitterness just yesterday. Elya had left. That meant he'd run away to study.

With deep longing and a burning pain in his soul, Itzkowitz went over to the window, pressed his forehead against the cold glass, and gazed out at the street. It appeared to him that everything was dead—the street, the sky, the little houses; they all looked dead, lifeless. In his soul, too, he felt, everything had died—past, present, future.

Then suddenly, in the very midst of his despairing thoughts and feelings, something bright flashed in his mind. He remembered that here in this very house, in the attic, his grammar text lay hidden somewhere, the book that held all the dreams, hopes, and expectations he'd had for his future. He realized there was still a very thin thread tying him to the past, and he wanted to run upstairs to the attic—immediately, this very minute!—to get hold of the precious, beloved book, peer inside, press it to his heart, and find within it an answer to his life, to all his lost hopes.

"Ma'am, I forgot a little comb in my room upstairs. I'm going up to look for it," he said quickly, and without waiting for an answer, he ran upstairs to the attic. From beneath the bricks, he removed the hidden grammar textbook and the New Testament. He pressed the grammar book to his lips and with tears in his eyes, he murmured, "I have only you left, you alone in the whole wide world."

He opened the book and began to read the standards of grammar that he already knew well by heart, and they seemed like the most beautiful poetry to him. He read about "subjects" and "adjectives," and he remembered how they had informed him about life, about the world; once again, they revived his dreams and hopes . . . and gradually, a fresh notion stirred within him: *Flee, flee from here*! he murmured to himself in feverish agitation. Flee to wherever his eyes would take him . . . chuck the cursed Miloslavka, the synagogue, all of it—and flee! Flee to Vitebsk. There, his friends would help him worm his way out of the quagmire, save himself.

He glanced at the New Testament and suddenly recalled the superintendent, that terrifying man with the terrifying face, though so warm and good-natured. He'd promised to support Itzkowitz, after all. Why not go and ask for his help, his protection?

He latched onto this thought like a drowning man grasping at a straw. The superintendent was the only person who could understand him and save him. All he had to do was go to him and relate what had occurred: how "they" had turned him into a yeshiva boy by force and imprisoned him in the synagogue. Ask the superintendent for advice, for help. The superintendent wouldn't say no. And most importantly, he might get a few rubles from him to be able to escape from here.

He placed the books in his inner coat pocket, rushed down the stairs, and left in a feverish huff, practically running to the superintendent at the other end of town.

24

That very same evening, Gershon the beadle was standing in the middle of the synagogue, looking about bewildered, repeating perhaps for the tenth time, "Where could he have got to?"

All day Itzkowitz hadn't been in the synagogue, and whomever Gershon questioned claimed they hadn't seen him.

Gershon remained in the synagogue late into the night, until, unable to wait for Itzkowitz any longer, he left for home, extremely uneasy. In these last few weeks, he'd become very attached to Itzkowitz, and now he worried whether something bad might have befallen him.

When Itzkowitz still hadn't appeared the next morning, Gershon's fear intensified. He ran to the rabbi, then to Isser, but no one knew anything. By the afternoon, the news that Itzkowitz had vanished had spread throughout the entire town. Various rumors and explanations began to circulate. At first, everyone linked Itzkowitz's disappearance to Elya's. People claimed they'd run away together, though where and why no one knew. In the evening, however, Elya's father received a letter. In the letter Elya wrote that he'd fled to the town of M. in order to study in a yeshiva. He'd fled in secret because he knew his father would never have allowed it. Remaining in Miloslavka, however, where one studied without a goal or purpose, was something he didn't want to do. His personal goal was to become a rabbi and in a few years' time when he reached this goal, he'd return home along with certifications for the rabbinate. The letter calmed Elya's father as well as the town. But now, the townspeople's mystification over Itzkowitz's disappearance grew even greater.

The next day Isser interrogated Gershon, asking detailed questions about Itzkowitz's conduct and riffling through Itzkowitz's remaining belongings. There wasn't much, but among the bits and pieces, Isser found a scrap of paper on which a few lines of an unfinished letter were written:

If my head were full of water and my eyes a well of tears, I would cry over my bitter fate day and night. If you were to know how unhappy I am! Not for nothing was I scared of traveling to this cursed town. I found here not a safe haven, but a prison. Even worse, a grave! The wolves who live here, led by their thieving rabbi, ganged up on me. With force they . . .

There was no more.

"Scoundrel! Lowlife!" Isser cried out. "He's run back to his apostates!" He hid the scrap of paper and showed it to no one.

In the meantime, the town resounded with various legends and rumors about Itzkowitz's disappearance. Some surmised that "evil spirits" had captured him in the middle of the night. ("We've heard of such things before!" they cried.) Others claimed he'd gone off to perform the rite of "suffering exile," voluntarily leading a life of wandering and deprivation as penance for his sins. Still others—these were the shrewder ones—whispered into each other's ears, "Listen. This entire story is somehow not so ordinary. First he's a tutor, then a *baal tshuva*, and now he's vanished. No one knows who he was, where he came from, or where he's disappeared to. Something's not simple here."

"I think so, too," the other responded. "Nowadays, if you dare say the words *lamed vovnik*, you get mocked; no one believes you. But it's possible, isn't it? We know there are thirty-six hidden righteous men in every generation. So why can't Itzkowitz be one of them? Where is he? He has to be somewhere!"

And, yet, others whispered another supposition to each other: "Did you notice the rabbi isn't saying a word about him? He's just silent and keeps sighing. Looks like he knows something . . ."

"And Isser? He's also unusually silent for some reason. Someone told me, very secretly, that Itzkowitz came to Isser in a dream. In the dream Itzkowitz, wearing his tallis and tefillin, said to Isser, 'Don't search for me. The time I was meant to be in your midst is over. That which I was meant to redress, I have already redressed. Even if you search for me in all the corners of the world, you will not find me.'

"Now you understand!" the teller concluded, and lifting a finger to heaven, he emitted a meaningful sigh.

25

Two weeks passed. The town had begun to calm down, to forget the strange person who'd whizzed through their town like a meteor and unsettled all of them.

One day, the superintendent came into the shop of his friend Zalmen Isser and abruptly asked him, his tone steely, "Where's your tutor? Itzkowitz?"

Zalmen Isser merely shrugged and said nothing.

"People are saying your community put him under cherem. That you excommunicated him and then drowned him. Ha!"

"Heaven forbid!" Zalmen Isser cried, frightened. "What are you talking about, honorable superintendent? What do you mean, drowned? How can you say such a thing?"

"Well, then, where is he? Where did he go?"

"No one knows. I swear to you, no one knows. He was sitting in the synagogue studying, and suddenly he got lost. We searched for him everywhere, but couldn't find him. No one knows where he is."

The superintendent suddenly burst out laughing. "But I do know where he is. Word of honor, I know."

"Well?"

"Ha, I'll give you your 'well.' If I told you where he is, you'd clutch your sidelocks and scream, 'Oy vey, alas, alas!' Hee-hee."

"Come on, sir, tell me already," Zalmen Isser begged with a sycophantic smile.

"You want me to tell you? Well, okay, I'll tell you. And in turn, you'll tell your community. Tell them, 'Once you had an Itzkowitz—and now he's here no more. Ta-ta. Flew away. There was once a Zalmen Yankelev or Chatzkelev, and now he's become Stefan Ivanich. So?"

Zalmen Isser turned ashen. "What does that mean?"

"Quite simple, little brother. In three days, we baptized him. Ha-ha! He's in the monastery now."

In this manner, Miloslavka's first step onto the road of European civilization came to an end. Nevertheless, that first step had been taken.

Glossary

Cheder (sometimes written heder): A Jewish school for children up to the age of bar or bat mitzvah (thirteen and twelve, respectively), where students are taught Hebrew, Bible, Talmud, and general religious studies.

Cherem: The most severe form of excommunication, occasionally used by rabbis in the past to sentence sinners.

Gemara: The latter part of the Talmud, offering rabbinical commentary on the Mishnah. Gemara is a major part of yeshiva study, and in-depth knowledge of its intricacies will earn one the title of *talmid chochom*, or Torah scholar.

Goy: A non-Jew. (Plural, Goyim. Goyish is an adjective of goy.)

Haskalah: The Jewish Enlightenment, an ideological, intellectual, and social movement that arose among Jews in Central and Eastern Europe. It was active from about 1770 to the 1880s.

Havdalah: A formal prayer marking the end of Shabbos.

Kaddish: An ancient Jewish prayer that is part of the synagogue service. (In this novel, the word specifically refers to the "Mourner's Kaddish," which is a particular form of Kaddish recited for the dead.)

Kvell(ing): To beam with happiness; bursting with pride.

Lamed vovnik (also called *Tzaddik Nistar*, "hidden righteous one"): One of thirty-six (the numerical value of the Hebrew letters *lamed* and *vov* equal thirty-six) righteous people believed in Kabbalistic Judaism, particularly Hasidic Kabbalistic Judaism, to exist in each generation. According to Jewish tradition, it is only in their merit that God allows humankind to continue to exist. The thirty-six tzaddikim are "hidden," concealing their righteousness from the world, often by being employed in simple trades (e.g., tailor, shoemaker, blacksmith, etc.).

L'chaim (literally, "to life"): A toast to drink to a person's health or good fortune.

Maftir: The section of the haftarah (text from the Prophets) that is read in the synagogue as part of the services.

Maskil: A follower of the Haskalah; a freethinker (Plural, Maskilim. Adjective, Maskilic).

Melamed: A teacher in a cheder.

Mensch: A decent, upright person.

Mitzvah: One of the 613 Biblical commandments; any good or praiseworthy deed.

Reb: Traditional Jewish honorific or title preceding a man's name (similar to Sir, though less formal).

Rebbetzin: A rabbi's wife.

Shabbos: The Jewish Sabbath; Saturday.

Sholem Aleichem (Literally, "Peace upon you"): A form of greeting traditional among Jews, equivalent to hello.

Tallis (sometimes written tallith): A fringed prayer shawl, traditionally worn by Jewish men during morning prayers.

Talmud Torah: A communal school where children are instructed in Judaism. May also mean a school for poor Jewish children.

Tefillin: Phylacteries; small leather cases containing parchments inscribed with Biblical verses, traditionally worn by Jewish men during morning prayers (except on Shabbos).

Yenta: A person (generally female) who is a busybody and gossip.

S. An-sky, pseudonym of Shloyme-Zanvl Rappoport (1863–1920), was a Russian Jewish writer whose prolific oeuvre includes plays (the famous *The Dybbuk*, among them), short stories, poetry, novels, and nonfiction. He conceived and directed the Jewish Ethnographic Expedition between 1912 and 1914; the thousands of objects gathered by the expedition bear witness to a lifestyle that no longer exists.

Rose Waldman holds an MFA from Columbia University. Her translations have appeared as a chapbook, "Married" (an I. L. Peretz story), in *Have I Got a Story for You* (W. W. Norton), and in various literary journals. She was a 2014 and 2016 Yiddish Book Center Translation Fellow.